MW00944256

THE GAMBLER'S MAIL-ORDER BRIDE

BOOK ONE

HEIDI VANLANDINGHAM

SHADOWHEART PRESS

The Gambler's Mail-Order Bride is a work of fiction. Names, characters, places, and incidents are the product of the author's imagination or are used fictitiously. Any resemblance to actual events, locales, or persons, living or dead, is purely coincidental.

The Gambler's Mail-Order Bride: © 2016 by Heidi Vanlandingham

Contact: Heidi@heidivanlandingham.com

Cover design © EDHGraphics

ISBN: 978-1543191530

All rights reserved. No part of this book may be reproduced in any form or by any electronic or mechanical means, including information storage and retrieval systems, without written permission from the author, except for the use of brief quotations in a book review.

ALSO BY HEIDI VANLANDINGHAM

For all Buy Links: www.heidivanlandingham.com

Western Trails series

Trail of Injustice (1)

Trail of Hope (2)

Trail of Courage (3)

Trail of Secrets (4)

Mia's Misfits (5)

Mia's Misfits is also in ABC Mail-Order Bride series

Trail of Redemption (6)

American Mail-Order Bride series &

Prequel to Mail-Order Brides of the Southwest

Lucie: Bride of Tennessee

Mail-Order Brides of the Southwest series

The Gambler's Mail-Order Bride

The Bookseller's Mail-Order Bride

The Marshal's Mail-Order Bride

The Woodworker's Mail-Order Bride

The Gunslinger's Mail-Order Bride

The Agent's Mail-Order Bride

WWII

Heart of the Soldier

Flight of the Night Witches

Natalya

Aleksandra

Of Mystics and Mayhem series

In Mage We Trust

Saved By the Spell

The Curse That Binds

Mistletoe Kisses

Music and Moonlight

Sleighbells and Snowflakes

Angels and Ivy

Nutcrackers and Sugarplums

Box Sets Available

Mail-Order Brides of the Southwest: 3-Book collection

Mistletoe Kisses: 4-book collection

Western Trails: 2-book collection

If you love historical romances, sign up for my reader list, and as a thank you, I'll send you the first book, a novella, in my Western Trails series.

To download, go to http://tiny.cc/nl-histwest

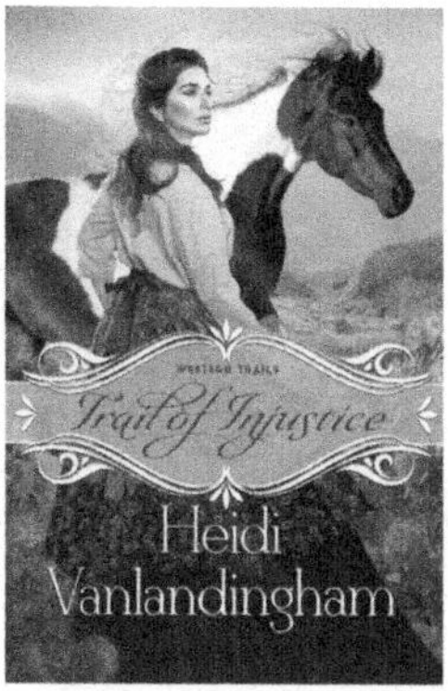

CHAPTER 1

Carlsbad, New Mexico, 1905

"Sheriff's lookin' for ya, Mr. Stone!"

Travis threw a quick glance at the young ragamuffin who scurried between the cramped tables in the saloon and skidded to a stop beside him. "He knows where to find me." Since arriving in town he'd laid low, trying to stay away from the sheriff and any possible trouble. No matter how careful he was, problems always seemed to find him—as well as bullets. He still hadn't figured out who'd shot him and had kept his eyes and ears open for any sign that someone from his old outlaw gang had finally found him. He'd walked away from that life five years ago and had worked too hard to get sucked back in because of circumstances he had no control over.

The wound had kept him in town longer than he'd planned, and he now found himself making excuses to stay. His gaze lingered on the young kid still standing next to him. The town, and a few of its occupants, were growing on him.

Looking back down at the spread of cards in his hand, his

right thumb slowly flicked the bottom edge of a card. He glanced at the other hands already on the table, then placed his cards face up near the pile of money. He leaned back in his chair and ran his thumb and first two fingers down his long mustache in a well-practiced motion.

His gaze touched on the five men sitting across from him. "I believe I have the winning hand, gentlemen."

One of the players, a sallow-faced kid with a scar on one side of his face and a lazy eye, grumbled and pushed away from the table without looking at anyone. His boots clumped loudly across the wood planked floor as he stomped out of the saloon. Two other men, the Cathcart brothers, stood together and planted their palms on the tabletop, faces flushed and eyes radiating anger as they glared at him—both with a pair each, fours and fives.

Jacob Smithton sat across from him and chomped on his short cigar. In his frustration, his blunt, yellowed teeth bit through it. The lit end fell into his lap and he quickly brushed it to the floor. Smithton's large body twisted as he ground the cigar into the wood, his hard gaze never leaving Travis's face.

"Not gonna let you take my hotel, Stone," Smithton growled, his fat fingers thumbing the edges of the cards lying face-up under his hand and showing a pair of eights. "You cheated me out of it, and I aim to get it back. One way or another."

Travis shrugged one shoulder and leaned back against his chair, the dry wood creaking underneath his weight. "Then you shouldn't have wagered it. We've been over this several times, Smithton. Hotel's mine. You lost it fair and square."

"Damn you, Stone!" The last player, a thin, gangly man, barked in a cold British accent…yet his clothes looked like the outfit of a hard-working cowboy, even down to the saddle-worn boots. "No man's that lucky."

"Don't reckon' I'd call that hand lucky, boys," a low, steady voice said behind Travis. "Dead man's hand. Been sheriff a long time. Only pain and death comes with that hand."

Travis pulled out a handful of bills from the pile and tossed them to the table in front of the brothers as the other men left the table. "Take that to your mother. Emily works too hard for the two of you to throw it away playin' cards."

Will Cathcart jerked back as if he'd been struck, his already florid face darkening to an unhealthy red as he shoved the money away. "Don't need your scorn, Stone." He grabbed his younger brother's elbow and pulled him away from the table. "We'll get even, Stone. Mark my words...we'll get even."

Travis watched the two men barrel their way through the saloon doors. Reaching across the table, he picked up the money and held it out to the sheriff. "Meant what I said about Emily. She's a hard worker. She deserves better than to have those two no-account sons of hers throw it away. Tell her to find a better hiding place for her wages—unless she's handing it to them herself."

Sheriff Tom Higgins took the bills, folded them in half, and tucked the money into his vest pocket. "Doesn't seem to matter where she puts it; they find it anyway. I'll talk to her about it." Tom's gray hair stuck out from underneath the stained brown hat, which was pushed slightly back on his head. He narrowed his gray eyes. "Not like a gambler to give away winnings. You surprise me, Stone." He grabbed one of the chairs and turned it around, straddling the seat. Resting his thick forearms on the top rung of the chair's back, he leaned forward.

"We need to talk, you and me."

Travis kept a steady gaze on the imposing man facing him. He liked Tom, which was unusual for him. Normally, he didn't stay in a town long enough to get to know anyone, much less the sheriff. He'd play for one or two nights then leave. Whether he won or lost didn't matter. Gambling from town to town was his chosen way of life, and he'd always enjoyed it.

Since arriving in Carlsbad, however, he'd begun questioning that choice. The town was growing, and good people lived here. He scrubbed the back of his neck, stretching the stiff muscles. Could he really fit in? Would his past let him?

He pocketed the coins and tucked the bills into his worn leather wallet, then slid the wallet back into the special pocket he'd sewn inside his coat. Leaning back in his chair, he stared at Tom, hoping the sheriff was just fishing for information. On several previous occasions, the lawman had stated he thought Travis looked familiar, and each time Travis was able to put him off. Maybe he'd finally figured it out?

"Levi delivered your message almost a week ago, Sheriff." He nodded toward the young boy, who'd never moved from his side. "Expected you to stop by sooner." From the corner of his eye, he saw the kid's tousled head bobbing up and down in agreement. He bit back his smile and waited for the inevitable—for the sheriff to tell him to leave town. Evidently, he'd overstayed his welcome in this sleepy town.

"Smithton's been at my office daily since he lost the hotel—sometimes twice a day. Keeps insisting you swindled him out of the Palace," the sheriff said.

Travis opened his mouth but closed it again when Tom held up his hand. "I've watched you since the first day you arrived, Stone, which you probably know. I make it a point to watch anyone who all but lives in a saloon." The older man shook his head, speculation gleaming in his eyes. "I know I've said it before...you seem so familiar to me, but damned if I can figure out why."

Travis shrugged, schooling his features to remain blank.

"I just have that kind of face." Tom Higgins was smart, smarter than anyone he'd come across since he'd taken up gambling at the age of fifteen in hopes of escaping the Outlaw Trail he'd found himself living on after killing his father. He wasn't too concerned about the sheriff...yet. Travis had worked hard to bury his many mistakes. He'd somehow managed to create a new life for himself, and no one, not even a sheriff as fair as Tom Higgins, was going to take that from him. No one.

To calm his nerves, he reached for the cards and shuffled. Pulling a section from the back, he gave a well-practiced, smooth flick of his wrist and sifted them back together. He met the sheriff's gray gaze and raised the deck. "Friendly game? No wagers."

Tom nodded, his gaze following the cards as Travis dealt five cards to them both, placing the remaining cards face down in the center of the table. Travis glanced at his cards and rearranged them, placing the two queens side by side and keeping a seven of spades.

Tom discarded two cards and waited, no emotion on his face. "Like you, I've done this job for a long time, son. I'm good at it, too."

Travis discarded the two cards he didn't want and pulled two more from the deck. He'd drawn another queen and, as luck would have it, the seven of hearts. He now had a full house. Glancing up at Tom, he nodded.

Tom stared at his hand a moment then placed them, face down, on the table. "I fold."

Travis spread his cards out on the table for the sheriff to see. "I don't cheat, Tom."

Higgins stood, straightening the gun holstered on his hip. "Never said you did, Stone." He smiled. "Smithton wants his hotel back. Don't rightly understand why, though. He's run it into the ground. Place is so filthy, no respectable person will stay there. Can't give away a room." He chuckled. "Livery's cleaner than that hotel." He took a few steps toward the door then stopped, turning his head back to Travis. "I suggest you figure out what you're gonna do quick like, because Smithton's stirring up trouble. And I don't want trouble in my town, Stone. You best watch your back."

When the sheriff had gone, Levi leaned his elbows on the table. "Whatcha gonna do, boss?"

Travis bit back a smile. No matter what he did, the boy stuck to him like a shadow at high noon. From what little Levi would say about his past, Travis got the impression the eleven-year-old had no family. Like himself, the kid was alone. "Stop calling me that. I'm not your boss."

Levi nodded. "Yessir." His nervous gaze skittered around the almost empty room. The only people left were two Mexicans drinking beer at a table near the back door. "Well, boss? Any ol' answer would be kinda nice. Whatcha gonna do?"

Travis sighed and gulped the last of the amber liquid, then set the empty glass on the table. Standing, he pulled the bottom corner of his coat over his pistol and tossed a few coins on the table for the beer. "About what?"

Levi rolled his eyes and followed him from the saloon. They walked down the wooden sidewalk separating the business fronts from the dirt street. "The hotel. Sheriff's right, you know. The Palace is a mess. I think there's more dirt inside than there is in the street. And it stinks, too!"

Travis glanced down at his small companion, half listening as the kid prattled on. Tall and scrawny for his age, Levi could gain thirty pounds and still be too thin. He frowned, wondering when the boy had last eaten, and mentally kicked himself for not paying more attention. Nor had he noticed the state of Levi's clothes. The hems of his pants were more than an inch above his ankles and he had large holes at both knees. His shirt wasn't much better, with several buttons missing—one in the middle of his chest, as well as each cuff, which flapped around the middle of his forearms. The kid's boots were even worse. His big toes stuck out through aged holes at the tips, digging into the dirt with each step.

"What do you think I should do?" Travis asked, steering him toward the general store.

Levi's eyes widened. "You're askin' me for my opinion?"

Travis nodded.

With a serious frown, Levi twisted his mouth in thought. "Well, sir, I believe you need a woman. Womenfolk just got a knack for making things nice. My ma used to make our soddy sparkle—and that was nothin' but dirt! Problem is, there aren't many females in Carlsbad left—most of 'em are already taken. Those who aren't...well, you've done made 'em mad."

Travis stared at the kid, his lungs fighting to pull in enough air. A woman was the last thing he needed or wanted. He'd sworn off females after his mother ran off, leaving him with a father who'd cared more about his next drink than raising his son.

They'd stopped in front of the general store. Forcing his feet to move, he steered Levi through the store's front door. Fifteen minutes later, with a lot of help from the store owner, he'd managed to find two pair of jeans and two shirts. For some strange reason, Levi had insisted on a dark blue-on-blue striped shirt, almost an exact replica of Travis's, as well as a cream shirt.

Reaching to an overhead shelf, Travis pulled down a pair of brown boots, and the boy's small face lit up in a wide grin. Plopping down on the floor, Levi jerked off the ragged boots and stuffed his bare feet into the new ones. His shoulders drooped as his smile turned upside down. "They're too small."

Travis shook his head, fighting his own smile. He grabbed another pair and set them on the floor beside Levi. "So, you try on a larger size." He chuckled when one of the too-small boots flew across the narrow aisle, the other quickly following. Before Levi could shove his filthy foot into the new boot, Travis raised his hand. "Hold on a minute." He reached over and grabbed a pair of wool socks and tossed them between Levi's legs. "Put those on first."

Levi scowled. "Why do I have to wear socks? Do just fine without 'em."

"Well, men wear socks—and you'll soon be a man, so you should get used to them now. Besides, what would happen if, by chance, I take you riding one day and your horse goes lame? Ever walked a lot of miles?" Levi shook his head. "I have. Even with socks, I had blisters. Lots of them. Hurt like the dickens for days."

Levi's eyes widened and, with a nod, pulled on the socks, which were followed by the boots. He jumped up and paced back and forth down the aisle. Turning around, he made his way back to stand in front of Travis. Without warning, the boy threw his arms around Travis's waist, burying his face in his shirt. Not knowing quite what to do, Travis awkwardly patted Levi's trembling shoulders.

Levi raised his tear-stained face, a weak smile hovering over his lips. "Thank you, sir. No one's ever been so nice to me before."

What felt like a fist tightened around his heart, and Travis returned the kid's smile, a calmness settling inside him. "My name is Travis, not sir or boss." He tousled Levi's already messy, not to mention dirty, blond hair. He reached over and grabbed another pair of socks, and added several pairs of drawers to the growing pile. He paid the clerk, who wrapped everything in brown paper and tied it with string. Carrying the parcel under his arm, Travis stepped out onto the sidewalk with Levi scooting through the door right behind him.

"Now, how about something to eat? Are you hungry?"

Levi nodded. "I'm starving!"

"Good. Let's go to O'Darby's. Mabel's special today is her delicious peach cobbler."

"I've never had peach cobbler...what's cobbler?"

Travis chuckled. "Well, I guess you'll just have to eat your meal and find out."

They settled inside the restaurant at a corner table so Travis could watch the door. Several minutes later, steaming plates were placed in front of them. He watched the kid in disbelief. He'd never seen anyone devour a huge piece of fried chicken as fast as Levi. "Slow down, kid. You're gonna choke if you keep shoveling your food in that fast."

Levi swiped the back of his hand across his mouth, and Travis handed him a napkin. Levi stared at it a moment, then wiped his mouth again and set the napkin on the table beside him. "Can I ask you a question, Travis?" Travis nodded, and Levi's eyes dropped to his almost empty plate. "Why are you being so nice to me? I mean, I'm grateful an' all, especially for the clothes, but why are you doin' this? Do I gotta pay you back somehow?"

A kernel of unease settled in Travis's gut, and he noticed the way Levi slunk down in his chair. He lifted his hand to reach for his glass of water, and Levi's thin body flinched as if struck. The kernel blossomed into full-fledged anger. "Look at me, Levi." He waited for the kid to raise his gaze, which took longer than he liked. He hadn't seen this side of Levi before, and he didn't like it. Finally, Levi's dark brown eyes met his, and they were filled with fear.

Travis pulled his hand away from the glass, abandoning his drink. "Who hurt you, Levi? Was it someone in Carlsbad?"

The boy shrugged, his lips pressed tightly together.

"Fine. You don't have to tell me until you're ready, but if anyone, and I mean anyone, tries to again, you *will* tell me. Do you understand, Levi?" Levi nodded once. "I bought you the clothes because you needed them. You've taken good care of me since I arrived in town, so now it's my turn to return the favor. From now on, you can eat with me so I know you're getting enough food. That's what friends do for each other."

The boy's eyes widened. "You...you're my friend?" he said in a shaky voice.

Travis clenched his jaws and stared into the eleven-year-old's tear-filled eyes. "Yes, Levi. I am definitely your friend." He motioned for the waitress, who scurried across the room with two bowls close to overflowing with peach cobbler.

Levi stared at the bowl, his mouth hanging open. He picked up his spoon, shaking his head. "I've never seen a bowl so full."

Travis swallowed his bite, licking his lips with a grin. "As promised, Mabel makes the best cobbler in this part of the country, so dig in. It's even better when it's still warm."

Lifting his spoon, it hung suspended in mid-air. "I'm glad you're my friend, Travis. Really glad."

Frowning, Travis watched Levi shovel the dessert, spoonful by spoonful, into his mouth. "Are you even tasting it? How about breathing? Seriously, when was the last time you ate?"

Levi laughed and swallowed the last bite. He used the napkin to wipe off the circle of sugary peach filling lining his mouth and shrugged. "Yesterday I think. Sometimes Sam over at the saloon gives me any leftovers when he closes." He leaned back in his chair, his eyebrows rising. He rested his head on the back of his chair like he was going to sleep.

Travis frowned as Levi's lips slowly turned up in a devilish grin.

Suddenly, the eleven-year-old scooted forward, his chest pressing against the table's edge. "Travis, I know how to get you a woman...for the Palace, of course. You're gonna write a letter explainin' what you need her for—hold on a sec!" He hopped from the chair and grabbed a newspaper someone had left on a nearby table. Hurrying back to their table, he opened it up quickly scanning each page.

"You can read?" Travis asked amazed to see how fast the boy turned the pages.

Levi nodded, never taking his eyes from the paper. "Sure I can. Ma taught me before she passed." Suddenly, he pointed a dirty finger at a short advertisement, the heading in bold letters. *Wanted: Mail-Order Bride.*

CHAPTER 2

Chattanooga, Tennessee

"Mama!" Stella McCord called out as she pushed open the front door to her family's home...only to be greeted by silence. She walked into the front parlor, pulling off her gloves. "Mama, has the post arrived?"

She unwound the strings of her small satchel from her wrist and laid it on the entry table as she'd done a thousand times before, her gaze staring into the empty dining room on the other side of the parlor. The delicious scent of cinnamon and nutmeg filled her nostrils. An uneasy feeling skittered through her as she walked through the room toward the kitchen. Her mother would never leave the house with something in the oven. Wherever could she be?

"Mama, where are you?" As she rounded the wall separating the parlor from the kitchen, the washroom door opened and her stepmother stepped out with an easy smile on her beautiful face.

"Stella! You're home earlier than I expected." Lucie

McCord's smile quickly turned into a frown. "Is something wrong at the hotel?"

"No, Mama. Charles showed up an hour early, muttering something about his pesky wife. At this time of day, the front desk doesn't need two people manning it. There's barely enough work to keep one person occupied."

Lucie gave her a quick nod and picked up the dishtowel lying on top of the white porcelain oven. "Mmm, the cake is almost done."

Stella's stomach growled, and she laughed. "Not soon enough, evidently. I'm starving!"

Her mother returned Stella's smile. "Charles adores his wife. I think he just enjoys complaining. There's leftover meatloaf from last night's dinner. I can warm some up for you. Why didn't you eat at the hotel?"

Stella grimaced. "The chef served veal cutlets...slimy and undercooked. He's no more a chef than I am. Are you and father certain he trained in Paris? Personally, I believe he lied. It's sad. The hotel hasn't been the same since Grandma died and Cook left." She sighed.

"I know, darling. I miss Martha too. It's hard to believe she's been gone a year now. It's still difficult for your father to accept it. For a long time, it was only the two of them... letting her go hasn't been easy."

Stella sat at the table, watching while her mother gracefully moved about the kitchen, readying her meal. "I think she lost her will to live. After John died, Grandma told me those nine years of marriage were the happiest years of her life." She accepted the plate from her mother. Picking up her fork, she savored the rich aroma of the meat and buttered potatoes. Catching her mother's gaze, she wiggled her brows. "Maybe you should take over the hotel kitchen."

Lucie laughed. "Thank you, but no. I have enough to do here as it is. As you well know, your brothers keep me quite busy."

She pulled the cake from the oven and set it on the stovetop to cool. Glancing at the clock, she poured coffee into two cups and carried them to the table. "Speaking of your brothers, Wyatt and Mark should be home soon—unless it's like yesterday and they have to stay after school again." She pulled a chair away from the table and sat, an expectant look on her face.

Stella took another big bite, chewing slowly. Her mother was an excellent cook. Her own cooking was edible, but she couldn't figure out why hers never tasted quite the same.

"Stella?"

She sighed, laid the fork across the rim of her plate, and dropped her hands into her lap. She knew her mother wouldn't stop pressing until she got an explanation. "Yes, Mama?"

"Every day for the last fortnight, you have inquired about the post. When are you going to tell me why?"

Stella stared down at her clasped fingers, the knuckles white. She forced her hands to relax, and looked into her mother's clear hazel gaze. Stella was only six years old when seventeen-year-old Lucie and her younger brother, Alex, came into their lives. Her own mother had run off, leaving her and her father to pick up the pieces of their shattered family. In her heart, she loved Lucie. She was beautiful inside and out, and a mother to Stella in every way.

Her loud sigh puffed her cheeks out. "I'm waiting for a letter."

"Obviously."

Stella sipped at her coffee, avoiding her mother's heavy gaze. "I will be twenty next February, and have no prospects for a husband. I have yet to even be asked to a social event."

Lucie smiled. "There's no reason for you to rush into marriage."

Stella set the coffee cup down and swiped at the large

drop of dark liquid that had sloshed from her cup. "No man in Chattanooga would ever dream of considering me as a potential wife. Even after all these years, my reputation is less than flattering, I'm afraid."

Her mother pinched her lips together, the corners defying her efforts as they continued to rise. Her bright laughter filled the house, lifting the somber weight on Stella's shoulders.

Stella shrugged and rolled her eyes, a tiny smile playing over her own mouth. "I *was* a little heathen—even after you came into my life." Her smile widened. "The Singleton's never did forgive me for shooting their dog." She drank the rest of her coffee, relishing the sting of heat as it seared her tongue. In a strange way, it gave her the courage to continue. "Your experience as a mail-order bride was so successful, I decided to do the same."

Her mother's eyes widened. "Stella, are you certain? My circumstances were dire—I either accepted a bride letter or Alex would've had to go into a home for children. I couldn't let that happen. And yes, I was so very lucky…but if you remember, your father wasn't the man I was supposed to marry. That man died before I ever arrived. It was luck, and your grandmother's interference, that gave me such a favorable outcome."

"I know, Mama. But I need to do this. I *want* to do this."

Stella watched as her mother went over to her father's desk and pulled a cream-colored envelope from the top of a small pile of envelopes. Turning, Lucie handed it to her daughter and sat back down. Stella stared at the familiar flowing script of the owner of the mail-order bride service she'd contacted more than two months ago. She tore open the envelope and gripped the folded letter in her hands. After several disappointing responses from potential suitors, her hope was slowly dwindling...she'd begun to wonder if she was even desirable.

"Staring at it won't tell you what's written inside."

Stella met her mother's amused gaze.

"Go on, Stella. Read it."

Fingers trembling, she unfolded the paper and began reading aloud.

Dear Miss McCord,

I recently received a bride request from a man in Carlsbad, New Mexico, who I believe will meet all of your listed criteria. I have enclosed his letter for your perusal. Please let me know as soon as possible whether or not this gentleman is acceptable.

Sincerely, Adelaide Struthers

Stella snatched up the discarded envelope and pulled it apart. Another letter, much smaller than Miss Struthers', fell onto the table. She pressed the letter against her chest as excitement filled her. "I'm so nervous. What if...."

Lucie shook her head. "Don't think like that. There are thousands of men in this country. If this one isn't good enough for you, then you will just have to keep looking. The man holding the key to your heart is out there, waiting for you."

"Thank you, Mama. I love you."

"I love you too—now read his letter before I pass out from anxiety!"

Stella chuckled and opened the small piece of paper. The handwriting was bold and precise. She couldn't help but wonder about the man who'd written the words. She quickly scanned the letter, then slowly read it aloud.

"My name is Travis Stone. I am twenty-seven years old, and live in Carlsbad, New Mexico. I have never been married, and as you can probably surmise from my need to place an ad such as this,

I have no real experience with women. Growing up on the frontier hasn't allowed me that luxury. I have recently inherited a hotel, the Palace Hotel, and would be able to support you if you should decide to accept my marriage offer.

Sincerely, Travis Stone

Stella raised tear-filled eyes to her mother's beaming face. "He owns a hotel...."

Lucie clapped her hands and laughed. "It's a match made in heaven! Now you just have to tell your father."

"Tell her father what?" Sebastian McCord asked as he sidestepped his sons, who'd shoved their way around him trying to beat each other into the house.

"Wyatt! Mark! No running in this house!" Sebastian barked.

The boys skidded to an immediate stop, their expressions contrite. Stella didn't believe it for a minute. The second her parents' heads were turned, they'd dart off again at top speed. She'd seen it many, many times before. She shook her head, watching as her mother cut the still-warm cake. She put five generous pieces on plates and drizzled a sweet icing over each one. Garnishing each plate with a fork, she carried them to the table where the family now sat expectantly.

Everyone ate in silence, savoring the delicious dessert, but Stella felt like she was sitting on ants. The longer the silence droned on, the more she fidgeted, wishing someone would say something and take her mind off what she would eventually have to tell her father. Finally, she couldn't take it any longer.

"Mama, you're going to have to write down the recipe for Washington cake, as well as several other recipes, so I can take them with me." She slid her last bite into her mouth and slowly chewed, her eyes practically drilling a hole in the middle of the small white plate.

"Boys, go wash up and do your chores. Supper's going to

be a while, so go ahead and begin your homework," Lucie said in a stern voice. Chairs scraped against the wooden floor as they left without uttering a single word.

Stella swallowed, her heartbeat turning into a fast and almost painful staccato. A heavy silence filled the room again. She closed her eyes and let out a small sigh. Her father cleared his throat, and her mouth went dry.

"Stella, is there something you would like to tell me? From your mother's expression, I'm assuming she already knows what it is." Her father's low voice vibrated through her, and she could hear the fatherly push behind each word.

She let out another resigned breath. "Yes, Papa, there is. I've made a decision. Like Mama, I want to be a mail-order bride. The letter arrived today—and I plan to accept." She waited with bated breath for her father to explode. When nothing happened, she slowly raised her eyes. Her mouth dropped. Instead of red-faced anger, her father had a smile on his face. "You're not angry with me?" She cleared her throat, not liking how breathy her voice sounded.

He shook his head. "You've been moping around since your friend Penelope got married. I knew it was only a matter of time before you announced the same. Although I will admit, I expected a male to come courting first."

Stella jumped up and ran around the table, throwing her arms around her father's neck. "I was so worried you wouldn't approve of my decision."

His deep laugh rumbled through her slender body. "What kind of person would I be if I thumbed my nose at the very institution that gave me your mother?" He patted her back and gently pulled her away before nodding to the chair beside him. "Now, tell me about this man—who is he? Where does he live?"

"His name is Travis Stone, and he owns a hotel in Carlsbad, New Mexico."

Her father's smile faded. "New Mexico? That's more than a thousand miles from here...."

Lucie placed her hand on her husband's forearm. Even across the table, Stella could feel the wave of sadness coming from her parents. "She will be making her home a bit further than we expected, but we've always talked about taking a trip west. Now we have a reason." Her father nodded but didn't say anything, his lips a firm line on his face.

"Do I have your blessing, Papa?

He met his wife's soft gaze, and slowly the corners of his mouth lifted. He turned his head toward Stella and sighed. "Yes, sweetie, you have my blessing to marry."

STELLA READIED HERSELF FOR BED, her heart like a rock inside her chest. With a quick flick of her wrist, she turned down the pale green coverlet and sheet on her bed…but instead of crawling between the cool sheets, she sat on the edge of the mattress. She stared across the room, not seeing anything but memories. She'd lived in Chattanooga her entire life and loved it here. So why was she leaving?

"Penny for your thoughts?"

She met her father's dark gaze and sighed. "I'm afraid they're not worth even that much."

Sebastian walked into the room and sat down beside her, his hand resting over hers on the bed. He smiled. "I remember when I practically had to wade through toys and clothes to tuck you in at night."

"That seems so long ago—but at the same time, as recent as yesterday."

Her father squeezed her hand and nodded. "I agree. Welcome to adulthood. Your mother and I treasure every moment we've had with you. I just wish you weren't going so far away from us. We're going to miss so much—your wedding, children..." Her father cleared his throat, but kept his tear-filled gaze locked with hers. "We love you, daughter. Remember that this will always be your home, too."

She nodded shook her head, her own tears falling down her face unchecked. When she'd started this process, she hadn't thought about how difficult leaving her father and the rest of her family would be.

CHAPTER 3

Three weeks had passed since Travis accepted Stella McCord as his mail-order bride, but he had no intention of following through with that part of the bargain. Oh, he'd marry her, but she would never be his wife. Instead of landing a husband, she would get a job managing this hotel. Once this place was cleaned up enough for people to stay the night, his financial situation would improve. His hope was that the hotel would soon have a constant flow of guests, and he would find a buyer.

He spared only a cursory glance at the unused front desk inside the Palace Hotel as he walked toward it. He pulled up the jagged piece of broken wood that had once covered the top and threw it on the pile of debris in the center of the room. Grabbing the other broken piece, he used a hammer to force it away from the wall and frame where it was still attached. The wood wouldn't budge, so he grabbed a crowbar. With each jerk and push, he cursed his luck. He knew it was too late to back out now. This mess of a hotel was his, and he had to make the best of it.

"Travis! What do you want me to do with this?" Levi

stood at the top of the stairs, holding a box that was almost as large as he was in his arms. His unruly mop of hair and his eyes were the only parts of his head visible as he peered around the side of the box. "I found this in the last room. It was hidden at the top of the closet." He let out a loud bark of laughter. "If the shelf hadn't broke, I wouldn't have been able to get it down."

Travis groaned. "Great. One of the million other things I will have to repair. Just put the trunk down by the stairs, and I'll look through it later. It's probably nothing more than clothes. Come down here and help me with this..." he grunted, hitting the board again as he continued, "...stub-born...piece...of...wood."

Levi stopped and stared at the front piece of wood, his head canted to one side as he frowned. He squinted, his gaze focusing on the part still attached to the wall. He moved two steps closer and bent over, his hands propped against his knees. "Why didn't you just take off the outside board first? Whatever you're doin' with that bar is cracking it. You're gonna have to replace the outside piece now, too. Just tear into it. We can rebuild the front desk—make it prettier this time. This one looks like it was built out of wood from an old stable."

Travis let out a loud sigh and straightened, the strained muscles in his lower back complaining. He might as well raze the building and just start over with the luck he'd had so far fixing things. He wasn't giving up, though. This place was going to provide for his future. He glanced around the parlor with appreciation. This had been a fine hotel once, and would be again. Even with the patches of plaster missing and the damaged wood, he saw the beauty underneath the dust and grime.

Stella McCord was due on the afternoon train, and this place was nowhere near ready. It had taken him two weeks just to get the trash and broken furniture hauled to the yard out back. Once he'd gotten the hotel cleaned out, estimating the cost to repair all the damage had been easier. Unfortunately, it was going to cost more than what he had, so his time had been spent at the poker table more than here.

With his recent streak of bad luck, the woman would jump back on the train the moment she saw this dump. "Fine. Let's get this one down, and while I'm building a new front desk, you can cart everything in that pile out back to be burned later."

"All right."

"Want some help, Stone?"

Travis jerked his head around. The sheriff stood in the open doorway, minus his coat, with his sleeves already rolled up to his elbows. His bushy mustache raised in what Travis thought could be a grin, but it was hard to tell with all the hair covering the man's upper lip. "Figured you might need a few extra hands, so I brought some people with me." He moved aside as two women and another man walked into the room. All four of them glanced around, shaking their heads.

The taller woman settled her hands on her wide hips and clucked her tongue, reminding Travis of a surprised bird. Her hair was pulled back in a severe bun that gave her pinched features a strange, wide-eyed look. "Land's sakes, Tom, this is a might worse than you said. It's going to take a full week to get things put back together, and another day or two to clean everything!" She turned to the other woman and gave her a lipless smile. "Dorothea, we have our work cut out for us here, but I do believe we are up to the challenge, don't you?"

The younger woman nodded. She was petite, and not too thin nor too plump. Her dark brown hair was also pulled to the top of her head, but instead of tight and prim, it fluffed out more, softening her pretty face. Her wide-set green eyes met his, and her lips curled into a welcoming smile. "I'm Dorothea Smythe, the schoolteacher. My friend here is Alice Perkins. She is Reverend Perkins' wife. Would you like for us to begin upstairs? I'm quite certain every room will need a thorough cleaning before anyone can stay in them."

Travis nodded. "It's nice to meet the two of you, and I would very much appreciate any help you can give me. Do whatever you think is necessary upstairs. I'm not sure if Smithton kept any cleaning supplies on hand, but you're welcome to look around."

Mrs. Perkins peered down her long nose at him and gave a quick shake of her head. With a quick sniff, she raised her nose in the air again. "No need, sir. I brought all the supplies we shall need." She pulled Miss Smythe back through the front door. Just as quickly, they both re-entered with buckets, rags, brooms, and mops.

Levi, now standing behind what was left of the front desk, snickered. "They're in for a surprise when they get to some of them rooms. Looks like several families of birds and a few rodents have taken up residence." He glanced up at Travis. "Oh, and we're gonna need some cotton for restuffing the mattresses. Forgot to tell you earlier. That's where I found the nests."

The man who'd come in with Tom was leaning against the far wall, and let out a bellow of laughter. "I'd give two cents to see Alice Perkins' face when she finds those rodents. Dorothea teaches little boys, so she'll handle it in stride. That preacher's wife though..." He continued laughing and walked across the room with a slight limp, favoring his left leg. He held out his hand toward Travis who grabbed it in a quick shake. "Name's Ben Caden. We briefly talked the night you brought in your horse, but I haven't seen you in a while."

Travis remembered Ben, and had seen him around town a few times. He was a giant of a man, standing a couple of inches taller than Travis's own six-foot-two height. Ben had strong features with a ready smile. From the few strands of gray hair running through his black hair at each temple, Travis guessed he was maybe forty-five or so. He got the same easy feeling about Ben as he had the night he left his horse, Deacon, with him. He liked the man's relaxed, peaceful manner.

"Thanks for helping out. As you can see, I definitely need the help." He wiped the sweat from his forehead with his shirtsleeve. "I'm in a bit over my head here."

Tom clapped him on the shoulder and picked up a long-handled mallet. "Knew you would be, son. I warned you Smithton had let this place go to hell." He raised the mallet over his head and grinned. "Now, let's get to the fun part." Before he'd finished the word, the mallet came down and shattered half the front desk. Two more swings and it was nothing more than kindling. He leaned on the end of the handle. "Have anything else you need demolished? Need to work off some steam because of a few idiots who got themselves thrown in jail last night."

Travis laughed. For the first time since entering the building, he felt a kernel of hope spring to life somewhere deep inside him. "Anything broken that can't be fixed, have at it. To be honest, I was getting a bit worried. I have to pick someone up from the train station at four, and I wasn't sure I'd make it in time."

Tom's eyebrow rose.

Travis rolled his eyes. "Long story—"

"He's got himself a mail-order bride comin' in to help him run this place." Levi's chest puffed out. "An' it was my idea too."

"Didn't figure you for a married man, Stone. Or is it a family member?" Tom asked.

Travis forced his body to remain still, even though the

pressure to move was almost overwhelming under the sheriff's unwavering scrutiny. Finally, he couldn't take it any longer. "Have something to say to me, Sheriff?"

"Hmmm. Never expected you to settle down here, that's all."

"I don't plan to. Once I get this hotel up and running and making money, I can sell it for a nice profit. The lady is only going to help me achieve that."

Tom tilted his head to one side, his eyes narrowing a hair. "Does she know that?"

Travis shrugged. "Doesn't matter what she knows—or expects. It is what it is. If someone's desperate enough to accept a marriage proposal through the mail, then she must need to escape whatever situation she's placed herself in. This will give her a new start and a job."

Travis scowled down at the kid and pushed him toward the hallway leading to the small dining room and kitchen at the back of the hotel. "Go on with you. You can start cleaning up the stuff in the kitchen." Levi took off down the narrow hall. "And you can wipe down the tables and chairs in the dining room too!"

Ben stared at the open doorway down the hall where Levi had disappeared. "I've never seen that kid so happy. It's a good thing you've done for him. No one should be fending for themselves at such a young age."

TOM MET BEN'S GAZE. Something unspoken passed between them, but neither said anything more as they got back to work. They picked up as much of the trash and pieces of wood as they could hold and carried their loads to the back of the hotel, throwing it in the rapidly growing pile to be burned. Walking back inside after the second trip, Ben cleared his throat. "Has the kid told you yet what happened to his parents?"

Travis shook his head, mopping his forehead with his already damp sleeve. "Just that his mother died. Nothing else." He helped Ben pick up the last of the debris and headed around the building again.

"Didn't want to mention anything inside. Kid doesn't need to relive the story. No one should have to. His pa was shot and killed not too far from here by Jason Anderson."

"Anderson?" A shiver of foreboding stole through Travis at hearing the outlaw's name. Jason Anderson had been like a father to him in his early years. As a child, Travis had ridden with him several times, acting as lookout since he'd been too young to do much else. He shook the feeling off. That life was in his past.

"You've already met his kid, Clay. Tom said he stormed out of the saloon after losing several hands of poker to you—same day the Cathcart brothers threatened you. Kid's following in his father's footsteps. Raised him to be an outlaw. Clay never had a chance at a normal life." Travis nodded but didn't say anything, wanting to hear more about Levi. "Anyway, several years ago, Levi's father stepped between Jason and another man, drifter more than likely, who'd called Jason out for cheating at cards. Drifter was right of course. The only way Jason ever won was by cheating. Levi's pa took a bullet in the belly. Terrible way to die."

"What happened to Levi's mother?" Travis asked, unwilling to think about his own past anymore.

"That's what makes the kid's story so tragic. Not two days after the father's funeral, kid returned home from hunting supper and found his mother's mutilated body. Somebody had gone to an awful lot of trouble making it look like an Apache had done it. I know many good men who are Apache—scouted for the army. They were quiet and kept to themselves, unless they were with other Apaches. Then they'd have a grand time yukking it up with each other.

"Besides, Apaches didn't really take scalps. Early on, the Mexicans offered a bounty for Apache scalps, the practice taught to them by the Spanish. Even the French traded scalps for money. Far as I know, Levi was never told the truth. Army major who headed the investigation thought it best."

Travis shook his head, one side of his mouth curled up in disgust. "I never knew that—about the scalps. Always thought it was an Indian tradition. Did they ever find out who killed Levi's mother?"

"Nope. And probably never will. Sad, too. Poor kid has had to scrounge for everything—food, clothing, even a place to sleep. Womenfolk tried to help him, but he wouldn't have anything to do with them. You're the first person I've ever seen him get close to."

"Hmm." Travis didn't know what to say. Levi had been through something he couldn't even imagine. To find his own mother like that....

He grabbed the two wide pieces of wood he'd spent most of yesterday sanding and readying for the front desk and carried them into the lobby. Ben helped him measure, cut, and plane the planks until the seam down the center fit as if they were one piece. The frame was easy to nail together. In no time, they were done. After adding a second coat of stain, the two men stepped back and looked at their day's work. The front desk looked good. Really good. And surprisingly, Travis had enjoyed working with the wood. For his first project, it had turned out much better than he'd expected.

"Didn't you say you had to be somewhere at four? Tom asked, looking up from the floor where he was replacing several rotten pieces of wood.

Travis pulled out his watch and muttered. "Damn...Levi!"

The kid poked his head through the kitchen door at the end of the hallway. "Yessir?"

Travis sighed, trying not to roll his eyes in exasperation. Nothing he said would convince the kid to call him by his given name. "I need you to run to the depot and pick up the woman."

Levi scowled. "You mean pick up Miss Stella McCord...you know, your bride? If you're gonna marry her, you need to at least know her name," he muttered, but brushed off as much of the excess dirt he wore on his clothes and in his hair off as he could, then raced out the front door.

Travis could hear the women upstairs, beating and stomping as they cleaned the rooms. He'd already given up his room at the boarding house where he'd been staying, so he hoped they'd get at least three of the twenty-four rooms cleaned up by tonight.

Since the day he'd taken Levi shopping, the kid had slept on a makeshift pallet on the floor of Travis's room. It would be nice to give the boy a room of his own, something he'd probably never had.

He let his gaze slowly roam the lobby, trying to see it through a patron's eyes, and let out a cautious breath. They'd made a lot of progress today, and he was happy. But they still had a long way to go, especially with the wood, which was dry and colorless. And there was a lot of it: the stairwell, the squared columns on either side of the front desk, as well as the floor. He had to admit, the new front desk changed the looks of the lobby for the better—the place looked fancier already.

"The walls look like they're covered in soot. Think we'll have time to paint?" He ran the pads of his fingers over the surface, a gray film covering the pads of his fingers. He rubbed them together to get it off, then swiped his hand against his jeans for good measure.

"This room used to be a pale yellow, if I remember," Tom said, then moved to stand by the stair railing leading to the upstairs rooms. "I always liked it—made it look even bigger in here. The wainscoting wasn't as dark as it is now, and was more red than brown. A coat of varnish will bring this wood back to life with minimal work, too. With three of us working, we could have it done in two, maybe three hours."

"Good. Let's go ahead and wash the walls down so they can dry overnight. I'm hoping the ladies will be able to get at least two of the rooms done before they leave today. But if not, one more night at the boarding house won't matter. I'll get here early in the morning and start painting so we'll have tomorrow afternoon to do the wainscoting."

One brow rose on Ben's forehead. "Don't think you've thought everything through, Stone. According to Levi, isn't he picking up your bride as we speak?"

"And?"

Ben shook his head. "Correct me if I'm wrong, but bride means wedding...and wedding means you're gonna be a little busy tomorrow. Too busy to worry about this place anyway."

"I'm not going through any kind of ceremony. We will get married in front of the judge at city hall—"

"You most certainly will not, young man!" Mrs. Perkins admonished with a glare, her fists digging into each hip. "A marriage is a holy occasion and needs to be honored as such. The Reverend is free first thing tomorrow morning, so we will have your nuptials then. Be there at eight o'clock sharp. He has a bible study meeting at 8:30, so we will have plenty of time. Nothing fancy of course, but a marriage doesn't require any such nonsense."

Dorothea tutted. "Alice! Maybe Mr. Stone and his...unexpected...um...bride may have already had plans for their special day—"

"It's *not* special. It's just a regular day like any other," Travis interrupted.

Dorothea smiled. "Yes, Mr. Stone, you already said that. But I have to agree with Mrs. Perkins. Whether arranged or for love, a woman's wedding day is, indeed, special. To not observe it as such would be, in my opinion, an error. And not a very good start to your marriage."

"I really don't think a church wedding is necessary," Travis argued, but no one seemed to be listening to him anymore.

Alice nodded at her friend. "Excellent point, my dear Dorothea. Precisely that. Now, we will all be there as witnesses, and afterward, I think we'll have tea served with those delicious little cakes Mabel makes every Sunday. I'm sure she won't object, even at this late hour."

Dorothea smiled and clapped her hands together. "Oh, I love weddings!" She grabbed Alice's arm and pulled the woman's stiff body to the door. "Come on—we have so much to do before tomorrow!"

Travis scowled at the women's retreating figures as they hurried across the street. "Did either one of you understand anything they said?"

Ben and Tom shook their heads, frowning. "Nope. Not a bit," Tom said.

CHAPTER 4

Stella stepped from the depot onto the wooden sidewalk, her gaze moving down the right side of the street from where she stood, then to the left. Other than a lone wagon slowly making its way down the street, the only indication the packed earth was a street were the shallow ruts down the center. Staring at surrounding land, seemingly devoid of any life, her shoulders slumped.

She heard a shout and turned her head back to the right. She saw a young boy running in her direction. The tousle-haired youth skidded to a stop beside her and leaned forward, resting his dirty hands on equally dirty jean-clad knees. His brown gaze rose to meet hers.

"Are you Stella McCord?" he asked in a winded voice.

Stella nodded. "I am."

He rose to his full height, all five feet of him, and smiled. "My name's Levi, ma'am, and I'm supposed to take you to the hotel."

She frowned, glancing at the street behind her, then back at the youth. "Where's Mr. Stone? Why didn't he meet me?"

Levi shrugged. "Busy, I guess. He's waiting for us at the hotel."

The furrowed skin between her brows began to ache as her frown deepened. "He's waiting...at the hotel...."

Levi turned and motioned with a wave of a hand for her to follow him. "Come on!"

"Wait! What about my trunks?"

"They'll be fine," he hollered at her over his shoulder as he half-walked, half-jogged away from her. "We'll get 'em later."

Stella had no other options but to follow him, picking up her pace when he disappeared around a corner. "That's not how this was supposed to turn out," she grumbled as she tripped, almost falling off the sidewalk as she followed him down a narrow alley between the train depot and the building next to it. She stopped on the sidewalk and glanced around, unease settling in her gut. This town was so foreign…nothing like Chattanooga. From where she stood, dirt and rock surrounded her in all directions. The road was nothing more than the sandy desert floor. The only differences between the road and the rest of the land were the cacti and good-sized rocks scattered across the flat expanse. And more dirt. Everywhere she looked, there was dirt. Other than the cacti, her new world was brown.

Even though it was late afternoon, she could feel the moisture in her skin drying up the longer she stood in the hot sunlight. When she'd researched what little information she could find about Carlsbad, she found out it had only been settled about twenty years ago and was still growing. From what she could see around her, there were about fifteen buildings scattered over a few blocks. One day, if the town survived, it could become as large as Chattanooga, but she didn't think so. Who in their right mind would settle in a barren wasteland? She chuckled at that last thought. *She* was settling in this barren wasteland.

To her left, she saw another street running parallel to the one she was on. On that street, several buildings had been built. Two were large, Victorian-style homes, which she'd always admired. The two-story home's lush green clapboards were comforting, and added a splash of color. One corner of the home was a tower. She could almost imagine a reading nook in the downstairs section, and a small child's playroom upstairs. On the opposite side of the house was a large wraparound porch. The wood around the doors and many windows was painted white, along with the gables, porch columns and spindles. The delicate finials and crestings decorating the home were painted a pale yellow. It was beautiful. None of the other homes around it were as fine.

Shading her eyes with her hand, she stared at a three-story brick building at the far end of the street. She frowned. All of a sudden, she realized there was no Levi. She wasn't sure how, but in the flat area surrounding them, he had disappeared. Fists planted on her hips, her scowl deepened. Now what was she supposed to do? She had no idea where to go from here.

"Lady! Miss Stella!"

She blinked then blinked again to see Levi, plain as day, running toward her. Where had he come from? She let out a small sigh and shrugged her shoulders in a slow circle, the tight muscles loosening enough for a bit of relief. Maybe she was more tired than she'd thought? "Where in the world did you come from?"

Levi skidded to a stop in front of her and gave her a blank look. He turned and pointed toward the building she'd just been staring at. "There. That's the hotel." He turned his empty stare back on her. "Are you okay? I've been waiting for you to catch up, but you were just standing here."

She took a step toward him. "I'm serious. Where were

you? There's nothing between here and there! I couldn't see you."

He smiled and raised his brows. "I was sittin' down."

"Oh. Well, that could explain it, but you aren't really that short—and all I saw was flatness and dirt." She narrowed her eyes. "You were lying down, weren't you?"

His cheeks turned pink, and he dropped his gaze to his feet. "Maybe..."

She chuckled. "Ornery little thing. I'm going to have to keep my eye on you, aren't I?" With the back of her hand, she wiped off the drops of sweat beading on her forehead. "I *was* lagging behind. I knew I should've worn my riding boots instead of these stupid things." Raising her ankle-length skirt a few inches, she stuck out her black dress boots. "My mother wanted me to make a good first impression—and I listened to her, which is not something I usually do. My favorite boots were packed away in my trunk, and since I was only going to be on the train less than a day and a half, I decided to keep wearing these. Now my feet hurt."

Levi snickered. "That's silly. Men don't notice things like women's shoes." He stuck his hands in his front pockets and headed back toward the hotel, this time walking at a leisurely pace beside her. "They notice whether or not an animal is fat enough to eat, or if a horse is built for distance or speed. The men around here, mostly lawmen and gamblers—even a few outlaws—pay a lot of attention to mannerisms. You know, whether someone has shifty eyes or a tell when playing cards. Sheriff Tom once killed a man because he had a twitchy gun hand. Sure 'nuf, there was a wanted poster on him. Dead or alive. They got him dead."

Stella gave him a crooked smile. "You sure know a lot. How old are you? Twelve? Thirteen?"

He shook his head. "Nah, I'm only eleven. Just tall for my age, I reckon."

"Is Mr. Stone your father?"

Levi stopped and stared at her a moment, a wistful expression on his face that quickly disappeared as if she'd imagined it. "No." He turned and resumed his slow pace, but she still heard his whispered words: "But I wish he was."

Interesting.... Perhaps she'd jumped to conclusions too soon and misjudged Mr. Stone. She was still peeved with him, however, for not meeting her train. Sweat trickled down the middle of her back, and she swiped the palm of her hand across her forehead, wiping the sweat on her dark blue skirt, wishing she could remove her jacket. She wiped more sweat away as it trickled down the sides of her warm cheeks.

"Is it always this hot?" she asked Levi, who now stood just outside the open door of the hotel.

"Yep. Even hotter in late summer. You'll be able to fry eggs on a rock in half the time you can now."

Her eyes widened. "Surely, you're joking."

He shook his head. "It's the truth. I've done it many times."

She stared at his narrow shoulders as he walked into the shadowed depths of the hotel. The building was just a square box made up of red bricks. The outside needed work, as she took in several places where the bricks seemed to be crumbling away. Maybe a long porch would help break the monotony, or even an awning for shade. A few planter boxes on the lower windows would look good—if anything flowering even grew in this desolate land and abominable climate. Maybe she'd gather several different cacti. At least they were green.

Taking a deep breath, she knew she needed to go inside before Levi came back out to get her. Again. He seemed persistent like that. She smiled. The boy reminded her of her two younger brothers. Nervously smoothing her wrinkled skirt, she walked inside. It took a few minutes for her eyes to adjust to the dim interior. She blinked several times and found herself staring at Levi and three other men. All four were staring back.

The young boy glanced at the man standing beside him and motioned toward her with a jerk of his head. Stella's gaze moved to the man. She swallowed, unable to pull her eyes away from his handsome face. From the quick glance she'd gotten of the other two men, this one was the youngest. His brown hair had a soft wave to it, refusing to conform to the slicked-back style. The ends curled over his stiff shirt collar. The top three buttons were opened, showing smooth, tanned skin. Her gaze slowly lowered, taking in his tapered waist, trim hips, and long, lean legs. She bit back a smile. His boots were worn, unlike his clothes, and were covered in dirt. One or two more rubs and the leather tips would be nothing more than holes.

Her gaze returned to his face, which was chiseled and hard, as if he spent more time outside doing hard labor than inside. Underneath his thick mustache, at least what she could see, his lips looked full. *What would it be like to kiss him?* Her heartbeat picked up its pace as she forced her mind away from where it had been traveling, not quite certain she wanted to entertain any more thoughts along those lines. The man was very handsome...too much so, in fact. She usually didn't trust the nice-looking men. Because of her devil-may-care attitude growing up, they were the ones who made fun of her.

Someone cleared their throat, but she couldn't pull her gaze away from the man's amazing blue eyes

She heard the throat clearing again, and this time managed to pull her gaze away and glance at the other two men. The man standing next to the first man was older, maybe in his fifties. Twisting his hat in his hands, she noticed his thick gray hair, cut short, and a deeply tanned face.

Around his eyes and mouth were fine lines...laugh lines, her grandmother used to say. The last man was ruggedly handsome, with a few gray strands at his temples and the rest of his hair so black it almost looked blue when light from the window beside him shimmered over it. She could do without the smirk on his face, however. It irritated her.

"Gentlemen," she said, hoping no one heard the slight quiver in her voice. "Which of you is Mr. Stone?" Her insides quivered when the young, handsome man took a step forward.

"I am Travis Stone. You must be Stella McCord?"

She nodded, not trusting her voice as relief filled her. After several minutes of silence, she raised her eyebrow, glancing from one man to the other, the situation growing more uncomfortable the longer the men stared at her. She resisted the urge to begin tapping the toe of her boot against the floor by sheer determination, which was her strong suit. Her *determination* was well-known back home, and was partly the reason she was here. Finally, she took the initiative, unable to take the silence any longer.

"If you don't mind, I would love a tour of your hotel, Mr. Stone." She let her eyes roam the room, for the first time noticing the drab surroundings. Her misgivings about her decision to come to New Mexico were growing. "You're already renovating? Isn't this hotel fairly new?" Holding up her hand, she added, "While we talk, these nice gentlemen can go pick up my trunks at the station...since you didn't send Levi with a wagon."

Travis held her gaze a moment longer, then glanced at the men standing beside him and nodded. "Well, you heard the lady. Just bring the trunks here, and we'll move them upstairs later."

The man who reminded her of her grandfather now wore a lopsided smirk as he elbowed the ribs of the man standing beside him. "Come on, Ben. Let's help out the little lady." He turned his gaze to Levi. "You want to come along, kid? We could use another set of strong hands." Levi glanced up at Travis, who gave him a single nod. The boy turned his gaze back to the man who'd asked the question and nodded with a small grin.

"Thank you, gentlemen." Stella's gaze followed their retreating figures. The moment they disappeared through the door, she turned back to face her intended. "Your letter never mentioned problems with the hotel." She ran her hand over the smooth top. The wondrous scent of newly cut wood filled her nostrils. "This place is too new to already be falling apart."

"The previous owner didn't take very good care of it, I'm afraid."

His low voice rumbled through her. She liked how he sounded, almost cultured except for the faint gravel accompanying each word. She wasn't sure what to make of him, though. He seemed confident and considerate. She thought about the lack of a wagon for her belongings, deciding he was possibly a mite forgetful. She was used to people holding her at arm's length, scared of what she might do or say…but this man didn't seem to care, which was an entirely new sensation. She rather liked it.

Following him down the narrow hall, she stepped into a good-sized dining room. The tabletops had been wiped clean, as had the chairs around them. The floor, windows, and side table, however, were filthy. Cobwebs hung in long tendrils from the ceiling. The material hanging in tatters around the windows had once been curtains, but was disintegrating from the desert's harsh sunlight.

"We're in the process of cleaning and repairing. I was hoping to have a bit more done before you arrived," Travis said, stopping beside her.

"We?"

"Tom Higgins and Ben Caden, who you just met...well, sort of. The school teacher and Reverend Perkins' wife have been here all day as well. You'll meet them tomorrow. At the moment, they are probably harassing the town's baker in preparation for our wedding, and—I believe Mrs. Perkins called it a tea. Whatever that is. I prefer coffee myself."

Her mouth curled up in a quick smile. At that moment, Travis Stone reminded her of a petulant youth—and he was charming. "A tea is like a small party where people get together and enjoy one another's company for whatever reason. Yes, tea would be served, but also coffee and several different desserts as well. It sounds like a perfect idea, and will give me a chance to meet the townspeople."

He moved back into the hall and walked through the open door at the end, evidently expecting her to follow. "That sounds fine, I guess. Don't know much about entertaining, so I'll just have to take your word for it." With a quick arm flourish, he motioned toward the room. "This is the kitchen...I think."

"Oh my..." She pinched her nose shut with her fingers, quickly finding source of the disgusting odor. Two large piles of garbage had been thrown against the back wall. The narrow space was otherwise empty, except for a small sink on the wall to her left and a small table pushed up against the wall on her right. "How can meals be cooked—there's not even a stove!"

His warm hands covered her shoulders and turned her around, moving her back toward the lobby. "Let's go upstairs, shall we?" As if realizing what he'd done, he jerked his hands away and climbed the first step. With a small flourish of his arm, he waited for her to move in front of him.

At the top, she noticed the pristine conditions. "Oh, this is lovely!" The floor and walls were immaculate, with no hint of any cobwebs overhead. Peeking into each room, she noted the identical regular-sized beds tucked into one corner, and the small table beside each headboard. White porcelain pitchers sat on the tabletop, with the matching washbasins on the small shelf underneath. She inhaled; the air smelled like lemons, fresh and pleasant. "I don't understand," she said with a frown. "How can these rooms be so clean and the downstairs so filthy?"

"The two women I mentioned cleaned up here and left just before you arrived. We got lucky. Only a few of the mattresses needed new cotton stuffing, and Levi found a box full of quilts and sheets." He walked to the window and brushed the pad of his finger over the sill, then rubbed it against his thumb. "Not a speck of dirt left. After seeing the kitchen, maybe I should've asked one of them to clean it too."

"How many rooms are there?"

"Twenty-four. There are six along this hall, and six more on the other side. The floor above has the same floor plan."

"A good-sized hotel then." Stella moved to stand beside him and looked out the window. The view from here wasn't much better than she'd seen from the street below. A wild, rough terrain surrounded the small town, which seemed to have been built in a shallow basin. From her new vantage point, she could see what looked like hundreds of different plants sprouting from the desert floor in various shades of green. Surprisingly, small patches of yellows, oranges, and purples dotted the landscape as well, giving the area a strange, foreign beauty. She wiped the beads of sweat from her face with the back of one hand and sighed. "I miss the beauty of Chattanooga. The cooler temperature, too."

"I've only ever known the desert."

She glanced up at him, the sharp angle relieving some of the muscle tension in her neck and shoulders from the uncomfortable train ride. "You've never seen the Rockies, or the mountains in the east?"

He shook his head. "My earliest memories were of playing on a dirt floor in a small caliche house. My father had the brilliant idea to build a ranch in the middle of nowhere." His sky blue eyes met hers. "It didn't work." She liked the way the outside corners of his eyes wrinkled up when he smiled. His nose was nice and straight with only the tiniest hump in the center, giving him a regal look. Standing this close, she could see a faint scar running along his jawline, and her fingers itched to trace its length.

Stepping back, she cleared her throat, but he spoke before she could get the words past the lump that had formed. "You're probably starving. Would you like to go eat supper...with me?"

At the thought of food, her stomach let out a loud growl. She smiled at him. "I would love to, Mr. Stone."

"Travis."

Her smile widened. "Travis."

CHAPTER 5

Travis led Stella across the street, slowly leading her toward the restaurant. He didn't quite know what to think about the decisive-natured Stella McCord. She was beautiful, which was going to cause him many more problems. His lust, anyway. And did she have to be blonde? He'd sworn after the last girl to never get involved with blondes, yet here he was about to marry one. In name only, of course. The only reason he'd come up with this hare-brained idea was to make the hotel profitable so he could sell it and move on. There was always another town to see, and new games to play.

Holding the door open, he motioned for Stella to enter. He led her to his favorite table in the corner. The position enabled him to see the street through the large plate glass window, as well as anyone who entered the restaurant. Old habits died hard, and this one had saved his life numerous times. Ignoring the woman, he moved around the table and sat, his gaze meeting hers as she continued to stand expectantly.

He frowned. "Is there a problem?" Her full lips tightened

in a straight line, and her nose flared. Even annoyed, she was adorable.

"I know this was once part of the Wild West, but I was hoping that manners would still be practiced. Is it not considered gentlemanly to pull out a lady's seat when sitting at a table out here?"

An uncomfortable warmth spread over his cheeks as he scooted around the table and pulled out her chair. Once seated with her skirt neatly arranged around her, he carefully pushed her forward. He muttered under his breath and sat down again, staring at the red and white checkered tablecloth.

He swallowed his pride and met her questioning gaze. "I'm sorry. I haven't been in the presence of a lady in a long time. Please forgive my lapse of...manners." He silently groaned. *What manners*? Because of his previous life, the only things he knew to do with a woman were base and coarse. Definitely not the way to treat the woman sitting across from him. If his plan was going to work, he would simply have to do better.

"I don't expect you to treat me with kid gloves, Travis. How about we start by getting to know one another. Tell me about yourself."

He thought back to his own parents, trying to remember how they'd been together, but the memories were dark and hazy. Probably best they stayed that way, too. Trying to figure out what he could tell her, his gaze moved to the only other occupied table in the restaurant where an older couple sat across from each other. The woman said something and the man chuckled, his gaze fixed on his wife's smiling face as he reached across the table and squeezed her hand. Travis had never really paid attention to married folk, but now he wondered if he'd been missing out. Moving like he did was a lonely life—one he'd preferred. He had to admit, since taking Levi under his care, that preference had changed a bit.

He turned his head to find Stella staring at him. A flush of heat crawled along the skin on the back of his neck. Under her intent gaze, he wanted to squirm. Instead, he focused on the young Mexican boy slowly walking toward them, two menus almost as large as he was secured against his chest. Travis reached out, thankful for the distraction from his disturbing reaction to Stella. "*Hola,* Manuel." He took the menus from the eight-year-old with a smile. "Have you been working all day?"

Manuel's shaggy black hair fell into his eyes as he nodded with a toothless grin. "Mama needed my help today. She's payin' me with pie, too!"

"I'm jealous. Maybe I ought to go help your mama. Think she'd give me some pie?" Travis laughed at the boy's scowl. "I'm only teasing, Manuel. You can stop worrying. Besides, I like your mama's cobbler better. What kind did she make for tonight?"

"Cherry, *señor,* but you need to order food first. Dessert comes after."

Stella snickered. "Sounds like you listen to your mother, Manuel. My name is Stella. How old are you?"

Manuel threw back his shoulders. "I'm eight."

"You remind me of one of my brothers. He's the youngest, and is only one year older than you are."

Manuel's eyes widened, and his small body leaned forward. "Are they here too?"

She shook her head. "I wish they were. They live in Chattanooga, Tennessee with my parents. I've only been here one day, but I miss them already."

He nodded, his eyes filled with understanding. With a maturity well beyond his age, the boy stepped closer and patted her arm, which was lying on the tabletop. "I understand, *señorita*. I, too, know *soledad*...what's the word?" He frowned in concentration then suddenly his eyebrows rose high on his forehead. "Loneliness! That's it—I know that feeling well. When you miss your brothers, you come here and find me. I will help you like *mi madre*, my mother, helped me. *Si*?"

Lips pinched together, she nodded, her eyes filled with unshed tears. "Thank you, Manuel. I think you and I are going to become very good friends."

"What do you recommend for our supper tonight, Manuel?" Travis asked, changing the subject when he saw the tears in Stella's eyes. For some reason it bothered him to see her unhappy.

"The fish is very tasty. *Mi madre* cooked a sweet corn casserole, or you can choose carrots." He grinned, showing off his missing two front teeth. "I already know what you want for dessert."

"Then fish it is. I believe I would like the carrots, but I can't speak for Miss Stella on her choice." He glanced at Stella. "Corn casserole or carrots?"

"Definitely carrots," she answered without hesitation.

He stared at her a moment longer, a contented feeling settling in his chest. "Then carrots it is." He handed the menus back and without another word, Manuel turned and trotted back toward the kitchen. The smile on his face froze and slowly disappeared when he caught the wide-eyed expression on Stella's face as she followed the child's progress.

"What happened to him?"

Travis knew without looking what she was asking about. Mabel kept Manuel's hair longer than most boys so it would cover the ridged scars covering the back of his neck. He also knew they continued across his shoulders, the back of his arms, and down his back. He let out a soft sigh. "Mabel O'Darby and her husband own this restaurant. She's also the cook. Her husband rescued Manuel from his family's burning home when Manuel was about four years old. He was too little to remember what caused the fire, but he lost his parents and older sister that day. Mabel couldn't bear giving him up, so she and her husband adopted him. He was badly burned, and they almost lost him several times. . .but as you can see, he's doing well now."

"How sad. He seems happy though. I'm glad he's found a family who could love him, scars and all."

They enjoyed the delicious dinner, talking about the town, weather, and anything else that wasn't too personal. Mabel herself served their cobbler. After the small bowls were empty, Travis leaned back in his chair with a groan, rubbing his full stomach. "As usual, Mabel's cooking surpasses any praise I could give."

Stella chuckled. "I have to agree. My mother is an excellent cook, but even her cobbler isn't that delicious. Mabel must have a secret ingredient—"

"Travis! Travis!" Levi raced into the restaurant and skidded to a stop beside their table.

Travis reached out and grabbed the boy's arm, helping him stop. He then tried to hold the boy still as he bounced from one foot to the other, agitation filling the air around them. "What's wrong?"

Levi took a deep breath, then let it out. "We went straight to the depot like Miss Stella asked us to, and loaded up a large trunk and another smaller one in the sheriff's wagon and took them to the hotel. After we put them in the lobby, we finished cleaning the dining room and started on the kitchen. Ben seems to think it's missing a few key things to make it a kitchen though." Travis's lips twitched, but he didn't say anything and let the boy finish his long-winded tale. "Anyway, when we decided to stop and come get a bite to eat, the smaller trunk was gone."

Stella sat up straight, her hand pressed against her chest. "You're certain it's no longer there? Maybe one of the men took it upstairs?"

Levi shook his head. "I'm sorry, Miss Stella. Your belongings are gone."

"Nooooo..."

Travis glanced from Levi to Stella's anguished face. Tears pooled in her soft green eyes then fell, twin streams along each cheek. Even crying, the woman took his breath away… and tore his heart out at the same time. At that moment, she was the most beautiful woman he'd ever seen. Instead of ranting and blaming him for the disappearance of her trunk, she sat in stunned silence, crying. The sweet goodness he'd seen hints of since her arrival lay before him like an open book.

Reaching across the table, he pulled her small hand into his and squeezed, trying to reassure her, hoping it was what he was supposed to do at a time like this. He gave a stab at offering comfort like most men in situations like these, but when it came to women he was clueless. On principle, he stayed away from them as much as he could.

"Don't worry, Tom will find your trunk. In the meantime, I will buy whatever you need."

Her eyes glistened like the morning dew on spring grass, reminding him of the tiny oasis he'd stumbled on years ago in Arizona. He'd always planned on going back, but for one reason or another never had.

"Stella?" He didn't like her silence, nor the sadness etched on her beautiful face. He leaned forward, wanting to wipe the tears from her cheeks, but stopped the movement before he made a fool of himself.

"You...you don't un...understand." She hiccoughed and

pulled her hand away, swiping at the tears continuing to drip onto her lap. "That was my trousseau—my dress for our wedding. My mother helped me pick it out." She took a shallow breath as if her lungs couldn't pull in enough air. "The other items in the trunk, though, were even more special than my dress." Her chin trembled. "Those things can't be replaced—they were my grandmother's."

"Miss? Is everything all right?"

Travis glanced over at the older couple who now stood behind Levi, worry showing on their pinched faces. The woman stepped closer to her husband and slid her arm through his, her fingers curling around his thin forearm.

"We couldn't help but overhear a bit of what happened and...well...." The gentleman glanced at his wife, who gave his arm a small pat.

"What my husband is trying to say is we own the Myers Emporium, which is just a fancy name for the general store. We would be more than happy to help you out for your special day." She smiled up at her husband then met Stella's sad gaze. "You see, tomorrow is our wedding anniversary. I'm afraid the town's dressmaker is away visiting her family back east, but I would be more than happy to help." She held up her fingers, which were slightly twisted and bent. "These old hands may not look it, but they've sewn quite a few dresses in their day. I'm sure we can find something suitable for you to wear."

Stella's eyes widened. "Oh, but you don't have to—"

The older woman rolled her eyes. "Oh, *pshaw*. It's nothing. I want to help—think of it as my gift to you. Your wedding day should be special. And I hope your marriage will be as wonderful as ours has been."

Stella met Travis's gaze, her brows slightly furrowed as if she were seeking his opinion. He couldn't think of a single reason not to take the couple up on their offer. His last winning hand was quickly disappearing with the expense of her train ticket and the materials for the hotel. And he wasn't about to spend the five hundred dollars he'd stashed away for an emergency, especially if the sheriff finally remembered where he'd seen his face. He could only hope that old wanted poster had never been sent this far south. This quiet desert community wasn't a bustling city metropolis, but Carlsbad was growing, and he had the feeling his time here was limited.

He gave her a nod and smiled at the couple. "Thank you Mr. and Mrs. Myers. This is Stella McCord...my intended."

Mrs. Myers smiled, her cheeks wrinkling up in a cascade of fine lines. "Please call me Ida, my dear. How about you come by the store first thing in the morning, and we'll get you taken care of."

"I'm afraid Alice Perkins has set the wedding for eight o'clock," Travis said.

Ida made a shooing motion with her free hand. "Oh, don't you worry about Alice Perkins. I know for a fact that the reverend won't perform a wedding ceremony that early in the morning, especially if he has his bible study at eight-thirty as he usually does. Those women will show up at the parsonage a full fifteen minutes early just to gossip." She grinned. "And since I am one of those women, I will talk to the reverend myself. So plan on the wedding beginning at ten-thirty. That would give us some time to get you properly attired, my dear."

Stella gave her a shaky smile. "Thank you, Mrs....Ida. Thank you."

"Well then, that's settled," Mr. Myers said with a twinkle in his eyes. "Now, Mama, if we're going to be up at the crack of dawn, we'd best be moving along home. It's time for me to examine the backs of my eyelids." John Myers' voice boomed in the quiet room.

Ida snickered. "You were examining them before we left for dinner, you silly old man." She winked at Stella with a grin. "I will see you in the morning, my dear."

Travis chuckled at the couple's familiar bantering, the room's tension drifting away like a cool breeze. "There now, everything is fixed...well, almost everything." His gaze fell to his hand, still wrapped around hers. Shocked and somewhat horrified at his familiarity, he pulled his hand away and stood, the chair legs complaining with a loud *screech*.

He ignored Levi's smirk as the kid watched his clumsy action. He bit back a sharp retort, wanting nothing more than to be sitting in one of the saloons playing cards. How had his life taken such a sharp turn into insanity? What had happened to his dreams of settling down in that Arizona valley and living a quiet life—alone?

He sighed and shook his head, noticing how green Stella's eyes were. He turned in disgust, wondering where that idiotic thought had come from. He strode to the door, holding it open for Stella and Levi. The walk back to the hotel was done in a welcomed silence, but his internal monologue continued. When had he become such a coward?

Once inside, he and Levi picked up the large trunk filled with the rest of her belongings. With a few grunts and stumbles, they managed to get the heavy trunk up the stairs and into the last room in the north hall, which Mrs. Perkins had made up for Stella. Of course, the woman had no idea the room would be hers permanently…he had no plans to move her into his, which was unfortunately located directly across the hall. Their marriage would remain one of convenience, and he tried to convince himself that consummating their vows was the last thing he wanted to do. Stella McCord would be his wife in name only, whether she liked it or not.

. . .

THE EVENING HAD GONE from pleasant to disastrous in less than an hour. Stella longed for the peacefulness of sleep, and to forget. Curling up under the bright blue and green quilt on her bed and having a good cry was the first thing to do on her agenda. She couldn't think of a single reason why anyone would want her trousseau. There wasn't anything of worth inside, the items valuable only to her.

The loss of the beautiful robin's egg blue dress her mother had had made was upsetting, but the loss of her grandmother's things devastated her. She'd planned to wear the beautiful silver comb, decorated with tiny diamond chips, in her hair. It had been a wedding present to her grandmother from her new husband, John. It was all he could afford to give her, which made it priceless.

Stella didn't care about the porcelain tea set her mother had insisted she bring along—any pot could boil water for a good cup of tea. The mother-of-pearl inlaid frame had held the last picture her family had taken before her grandparents' deaths. But it was the necklace, though, that upset her the most. It was a family heirloom her mother had given to her just before she'd boarded the train.

"Here we are." They set her trunk against the wall out of the way, and walked back to the door. She sucked her lips between her teeth. Levi's movements perfectly mimicked Travis's.

"If you need anything, my room is across the hall," Travis said as he backed from the room.

She glanced around, wanting nothing more than to be left alone to wallow in her misery. "Thank you, but I will be fine." She held her body still until the door closed behind them with a soft *snick*. Her shaky legs immediately gave out, and she dropped onto the edge of the bed. Nothing on this trip had worked out as she'd planned. But Travis was more than she'd ever hoped for, with his quiet watchfulness and ruggedly handsome looks.

She walked over to the window, thankfully not really seeing anything other than her own sad reflection staring back at her. This place—what had she been thinking? Everything here was horrible. She'd liked Levi immediately, and Travis…well, he seemed nice. But should she marry him? It wasn't too late to back out, and she still had the money her father gave her for a return train ticket. She rubbed her arm, still able to feel the warmth from Travis's hand where it had lain as they walked back from the restaurant.

Her hands fell to her sides as she absently stared through the darkened window. As her vision adjusted, the only things visible were a few gaslights in the distance. Everything else was an impenetrable black curtain.

She'd gotten the distinct impression that Travis hadn't wanted a bride at all. He wasn't acting like a nervous groom looking forward to his wedding night. Instead, he seemed to hold her at arm's length…as if her presence was nothing more than a bother.

Forcing her legs to move toward the trunk, she opened the lid and pulled out the few items she'd need for the evening, and in the morning. With no wardrobe in the room, she'd worry about a more permanent solution for her clothing after the ceremony. If she managed to make it through the day. With a loud sigh, she pushed the worry away to think about tomorrow. With her nerves in a jumble, tonight she was going to cry herself to sleep.

CHAPTER 6

It was just after noon, and Stella stood in front of the long cheval mirror in the back room of the Myers' general store. The reflection staring back at her couldn't be her own—could it? Ida had somehow managed to artfully weave her blonde hair into a beautiful and flattering style. The older woman had plaited, twisted, tucked, and anchored the long strands against her scalp with close to fifty pins. Instead of the normal raised pompadour on top, her hair had been smoothed against her scalp with small curls around her face.

The pale purple dress was beyond stunning and accentuated her slim figure to perfection. When tight corsets had become the fashion, she had been grateful for her tiny waist. No way was she going to bind herself up in that medieval contraption, unable to move or breathe, when she didn't have to. She ran the pads of her fingers over the high delicate lace collar, the intricate threads woven into a beautiful pattern that reminded her of snowflakes. The upper bodice and long sleeves were made from the same lace. From her tucked-in waist to her knees, the skirt was narrower, then turned into fuller pleats falling to the tops of her white kidskin boots.

"Ida, this dress is magnificent—and much too generous. I can't accept this."

The older woman *tsked* behind her as she stepped away and looked her over from head to foot. "My dear, this dress was positively meant for you. Mr. Stone won't be able to take his eyes off you. I chose well; the light purple makes your complexion glow and your beautiful hair simply shines! I must say, I am thankful that Reverend Perkins delayed the wedding until two o'clock. That's given me enough time to make the alterations to your dress."

Stella turned around. "But—"

Ida gave her a stern frown. "No buts. I insist. The dress is yours. Besides, no one in this desert town would ever buy something so fine. Life here isn't balls and parties—it's dry and dirty. You'll see soon enough for yourself. Take a bit of frivolity when you can, my dear."

Stella wrapped Ida in a tight embrace, the woman's pleasant lilac scent filling her nostrils. "Thank you—for everything."

Ida patted Stella's back. "You are more than welcome. John and I never had children, and I've always wondered what it would have been like to dress my daughter for her own nuptials. You see, my dear, you've given me a gift as well."

Stella blinked back the tears to clear her blurry vision, refusing to mess up the miracle Ida had wrought. Stepping away, she smoothed imaginary wrinkles with her sweaty palms. "You will be there, won't you? At the wedding?"

Ida smiled and placed her hand on Stella's arm and gave it a gentle squeeze. "John and I wouldn't miss it for the world."

The closed door swung open with a loud *bang,* and they whirled around just as two women burst into the room. "We just heard the terrible news! What can we do to help, Ida?" the tall, severe-looking woman asked before jerking to a stop. The younger lady, who was shorter with a curvy figure, ran into her backside with a muffled *thump*.

"Alice! What in the world..." The shorter lady stepped around the woman evidently named Alice and stopped beside her friend. Both women were staring at Stella in wonder. "Well, my, my. Won't Mr. Stone be amazed."

Alice snickered. "I don't think amazed is the word I would use, Dorothea."

Dorothea's eyes widened, turning her head to her friend. "Alice Perkins! You're a minister's wife!"

With a quick eye roll, the tall woman shook her head, her hair pulled so tightly into a bun not a single strand moved. "I may be a minister's wife, but I'm still a woman. I know how men think. Mr. Stone is going to be knocked on his rear end when he gets a look at his bride." Alice stepped forward, her gaze moving from Stella's upswept hair and down to the toes of her boots. "My, but you've done an amazing job, Ida. It's as if she stepped out of one of your fashion magazines. My dear, you are exquisite."

Ida smiled. "Stella McCord, this is Alice Perkins. Her friend over there with her mouth hanging open is Dorothea Smythe, our schoolteacher."

Dorothea's mouth snapped shut, and Stella smiled. "It's very nice to meet you both."

Alice's arms folded over her chest. "Hmm, proper manners too," she said with a quick nod. "Your mother evidently raised you right."

"Alice..." Ida groaned.

The woman in question raised her brows. "What? It's only an observation. Besides, she's going to need everything she can get in her arsenal once she's married to Mr. Stone."

Stella frowned, glancing at each woman. "Excuse me? What do you mean?"

Dorothea waved her hand and stepped in front of Alice, pushing her friend back one step at a time. "Now, don't mind her. When we heard what happened to your trousseau, we raced from the restaurant, leaving it in a complete mess. Since you both have everything under control here, we'll get out of your way and return to our self-appointed job of preparing for the after-wedding tea." She pushed Alice back another couple of steps. "Isn't that right, Alice?"

The imposing woman jerked to a stop. "Why yes, it is." She grabbed Dorothea's arm and pulled her back through the door, muttering about the things they still needed to take care of as they left the store.

Stella let out the breath she'd been holding, although she had no idea why. "I feel as if I just ran a race. Even my mind is tired."

Ida laughed. "If that's the worst those two do to you today, I'll be surprised. They mean well, but you've just met the nosiest woman in Carlsbad. Dorothea tries to rein Alice in, but it's like lassoing a whirlwind. Impossible." She glanced at the mantle clock sitting on the shelf behind her sewing table. "Now, if we don't hurry, you're going to be late for your own wedding. Let me change into my Sunday best, and we'll be on our way. It will only take me a minute."

"I'm ready when you are." Stella smiled. For the first time since arriving, she believed it.

TRAVIS FIDGETED, shuffling the cards with a long-practiced motion, which he repeated several more times. Finally, he laid out everybody's hand and glanced at his own. He waited for the other men to discard the ones they couldn't use and redraw. Those who had even a nominal hand placed their bets. For the first time since he'd started playing that morning, he lost. Thankfully, he hadn't bet much, keeping most of the money he'd won—almost a hundred and fifty dollars. Considering the deplorable state of the hotel, he was going to need every penny.

"Travis, you gotta leave now. You need to get to the church or you're gonna miss your own wedding," Levi pleaded for the third time.

With a sneer, he tolerated the men's ribald comments and gestures for a few more minutes then stood, tossing the deck of cards onto the center of the table. "Gentlemen. Enjoy."

"You too, Stone! Bet you're gonna enjoy this evenin' a lot more 'n we will!" a scarecrow-looking cowboy hollered from the next table.

"Shut up, Thomas!" Travis hollered back. Amid the loud laughter, he turned and followed Levi outside, then down the sidewalk toward the church. His stomach clenched as his nervousness increased. He pulled at the stiff collar Tom had insisted he wear. Pulling out his pocket watch, he pressed the release catch with his thumbnail and flipped open the cover. Two-ten. His steps quickened. He really was late. The wedding was supposed to have begun ten minutes ago.

He climbed up the church steps two at a time and swung the door open. Several feet inside, his eyes finally adjusted to the dim interior. His steps slowed to a stop as he stared at the blonde vision standing at the end of the aisle. Stella was breathtaking. The dress hugged her slim figure to perfection. He felt his body tighten uncomfortably. Her large green eyes stared back, pulling him into their depths. Her cheeks turned a soft pink, and he wouldn't have been able to stop the corners of his mouth from curling up if he'd wanted to. She was adorable...and soon to be his.

A frisson of dread settled in his chest at that last thought. He didn't need the burden of a wife. He'd never wanted that inconvenience. Every woman he'd known was fickle and self-serving. Even his own mother had thought only of herself when she'd abandoned him and his father. It had been a harsh lesson to learn at ten years old—one he could never forget. Her leaving had destroyed his father, turned him into an even meaner drunk.

He forced the smile from his face and schooled his features as he walked toward the small group of people waiting to perform the ceremony. This was a business arrangement—an arrangement he'd failed to convey to his bride-to-be. He'd planned on telling her last night while they ate, but it had slipped his mind when Levi barged in with news of the missing trunk. As soon as they returned to the hotel, he would rectify the situation. He needed Stella to run the hotel—something he couldn't do—and nothing more.

The reverend didn't waste any time once Travis was situated between Tom, who was acting as his best man, and Stella. About five minutes later, the groom found himself shaking Tom and Ben's hands as they congratulated him. Levi, however, sat in the first pew, watching them with a wistful expression on his face. Travis smiled and with a quick wave of his hand, motioned for the boy to join them. Levi's face lit up, a wide smile replacing the sadness. Hopping off the pew, he hurried over and wrapped his arms around Travis's waist in a tight hug. Travis held him for a moment before leaning back to tousle the kid's hair.

Levi's grin widened, and he stepped away. Travis watched as he turned to Stella, waiting for Ida to free her from her tight embrace. Stella turned and smiled at Levi, her arms opening wide. Travis's heart thudded against his ribs, and he rubbed his fist over the spot. Levi wrapped his arms around Stella's small waist, his little face pinched as he hugged her, as if he was trying not to cry. Travis frowned. The last thing he wanted was to hurt the boy, but making sure he had food and a safe place to sleep had seemed so simple at the time. Now he wasn't sure he should've let him get so attached. The hotel, these people, even Stella, were only temporary. A means to an end for him. He sighed. He would have to sit Levi down and explain that to him. The kid was smart, and Travis knew he'd get through to him.

A sharp clap on his shoulder pulled his attention back to the present situation. Turning, he gave Ben a crooked smile. "Never thought in a million years I'd ever be married."

Ben tilted his head toward Stella. "And to a right pretty filly too." Ben's expression turned serious. He took Travis by the shoulder and led him a few feet away from everyone. "I've seen that look before on my own face—where you want nothing more than to run in the opposite direction as fast as you can without a thought to what you're doing or those you leave behind.

"My advice to you is to settle down. This town ain't bad. There's good people here. Now that you own the hotel, you could quit gambling. Not to mention Levi looks up to you like he would a father. You leave now, you will break that kid's heart. Don't do the same thing to him that your mother did to you. You're a better man than that, Travis."

Travis scowled. "How do you..."

Ben gave the small group of people talking behind them a cursory glance, making sure no one was paying them any attention. "You've been here what…six weeks?" Travis nodded. "So you were shot five weeks ago. Your horse brought you back to the livery. Doc said you'd gotten lucky—any lower and the bullet would've killed you. You couldn't be moved, so I told him I'd watch over you. After a couple of days, you started thrashing around, and Doc didn't want you to undo all the work he'd done sewing you up, so he gave you a dose of laudanum. And you talked." He held up his hand. Travis snapped his mouth shut and scrubbed his hands over his face, but stayed silent. "I haven't said anything about this to anyone. I believe you're a good man. From what I've seen, other than gambling, you've seemed to turn your life around. Why run and throw all that away?"

"What do you want me to say, Ben? I don't know the first thing about settling down—I've never known what a real home was like. I brought Stella here for one purpose and one purpose only—to help make a profit from the hotel so I can sell it and move on. I'm not the kind of man that stays in one place for very long. As a matter of fact, I've been in Carlsbad longer than any other town." Travis saw Tom move closer to Stella, dipping his head down to hear something she said. "Besides, it's only a matter of time before Tom realizes who I am—what I've done. I want to be long gone before that happens."

"Promise me you won't do anything rash. Think about Stella and Levi—and me. I'd like to think I'm your friend. We can figure something out."

Travis shook his head. "Law's clear on murder, Ben. Tom's already suspicious. He's too smart not to figure it out." He held out his hand, which Ben took with a look of resignation. Travis smiled. "I've never had a friend, Ben. I'd be honored to have you as my first." Ben's eyes widened as Travis shook his hand, then walked back to the others as everyone left the church.

Travis fidgeted, shuffling the cards with a long-practiced motion, which he repeated several more times. Finally, he laid out everybody's hand and glanced at his own. He waited for the other men to discard the ones they couldn't use and redraw. Those who had even a nominal hand placed their bets. For the first time since he'd started playing that morning, he lost. Thankfully, he hadn't bet much, keeping most of the money he'd won—almost a hundred and fifty dollars. Considering the deplorable state of the hotel, he was going to need every penny.

"Travis, you gotta leave now. You need to get to the church or you're gonna miss your own wedding," Levi pleaded for the third time.

With a sneer, he tolerated the men's ribald comments and gestures for a few more minutes then stood, tossing the deck of cards onto the center of the table. "Gentlemen. Enjoy."

"You too, Stone! Bet you're gonna enjoy this evenin' a lot more 'n we will!" a scarecrow-looking cowboy hollered from the next table.

"Shut up, Thomas!" Travis hollered back. Amid the loud laughter, he turned and followed Levi outside, then down the sidewalk toward the church. His stomach clenched as his nervousness increased. He pulled at the stiff collar Tom had insisted he wear. Pulling out his pocket watch, he pressed the release catch with his thumbnail and flipped open the cover. Two-ten. His steps quickened. He really was late. The wedding was supposed to have begun ten minutes ago.

He climbed up the church steps two at a time and swung the door open. Several feet inside, his eyes finally adjusted to the dim interior. His steps slowed to a stop as he stared at the blonde vision standing at the end of the aisle. Stella was breathtaking. The dress hugged her slim figure to perfection. He felt his body tighten uncomfortably. Her large green eyes stared back, pulling him into their depths. Her cheeks turned a soft pink, and he wouldn't have been able to stop the corners of his mouth from curling up if he'd wanted to. She was adorable...and soon to be his.

A frisson of dread settled in his chest at that last thought. He didn't need the burden of a wife. He'd never wanted that inconvenience. Every woman he'd known was fickle and self-serving. Even his own mother had thought only of herself when she'd abandoned him and his father. It had been a harsh lesson to learn at ten years old—one he could never forget. Her leaving had destroyed his father, turned him into an even meaner drunk.

He forced the smile from his face and schooled his features as he walked toward the small group of people waiting to perform the ceremony. This was a business arrangement—an arrangement he'd failed to convey to his bride-to-be. He'd planned on telling her last night while they ate, but it had slipped his mind when Levi barged in with news of the missing trunk. As soon as they returned to the hotel, he would rectify the situation. He needed Stella to run the hotel—something he couldn't do—and nothing more.

The reverend didn't waste any time once Travis was situated between Tom, who was acting as his best man, and Stella. About five minutes later, the groom found himself shaking Tom and Ben's hands as they congratulated him. Levi, however, sat in the first pew, watching them with a wistful expression on his face. Travis smiled and with a quick wave of his hand, motioned for the boy to join them. Levi's face lit up, a wide smile replacing the sadness. Hopping off the pew, he hurried over and wrapped his arms around Travis's waist in a tight hug. Travis held him for a moment before leaning back to tousle the kid's hair.

Levi's grin widened, and he stepped away. Travis watched as he turned to Stella, waiting for Ida to free her from her tight embrace. Stella turned and smiled at Levi, her arms opening wide. Travis's heart thudded against his ribs, and he rubbed his fist over the spot. Levi wrapped his arms around Stella's small waist, his little face pinched as he hugged her, as if he was trying not to cry. Travis frowned. The last thing he wanted was to hurt the boy, but making sure he had food and a safe place to sleep had seemed so simple at the time. Now he wasn't sure he should've let him get so attached. The hotel, these people, even Stella, were only temporary. A means to an end for him. He sighed. He would have to sit Levi down and explain that to him. The kid was smart, and Travis knew he'd get through to him.

A sharp clap on his shoulder pulled his attention back to the present situation. Turning, he gave Ben a crooked smile. "Never thought in a million years I'd ever be married."

Ben tilted his head toward Stella. "And to a right pretty filly too." Ben's expression turned serious. He took Travis by the shoulder and led him a few feet away from everyone. "I've seen that look before on my own face—where you want nothing more than to run in the opposite direction as fast as you can without a thought to what you're doing or those you leave behind.

"My advice to you is to settle down. This town ain't bad. There's good people here. Now that you own the hotel, you could quit gambling. Not to mention Levi looks up to you like he would a father. You leave now, you will break that kid's heart. Don't do the same thing to him that your mother did to you. You're a better man than that, Travis."

Travis scowled. "How do you..."

Ben gave the small group of people talking behind them a cursory glance, making sure no one was paying them any attention. "You've been here what…six weeks?" Travis nodded. "So you were shot five weeks ago. Your horse brought you back to the livery. Doc said you'd gotten lucky—any lower and the bullet would've killed you. You couldn't be moved, so I told him I'd watch over you. After a couple of days, you started thrashing around, and Doc didn't want you to undo all the work he'd done sewing you up, so he gave you a dose of laudanum. And you talked." He held up his hand. Travis snapped his mouth shut and scrubbed his hands over his face, but stayed silent. "I haven't said anything about this to anyone. I believe you're a good man. From what I've seen, other than gambling, you've seemed to turn your life around. Why run and throw all that away?"

"What do you want me to say, Ben? I don't know the first thing about settling down—I've never known what a real home was like. I brought Stella here for one purpose and one purpose only—to help make a profit from the hotel so I can sell it and move on. I'm not the kind of man that stays in one place for very long. As a matter of fact, I've been in Carlsbad longer than any other town." Travis saw Tom move closer to Stella, dipping his head down to hear something she said. "Besides, it's only a matter of time before Tom realizes who I am—what I've done. I want to be long gone before that happens."

"Promise me you won't do anything rash. Think about Stella and Levi—and me. I'd like to think I'm your friend. We can figure something out."

Travis shook his head. "Law's clear on murder, Ben. Tom's already suspicious. He's too smart not to figure it out." He held out his hand, which Ben took with a look of resignation. Travis smiled. "I've never had a friend, Ben. I'd be honored to have you as my first." Ben's eyes widened as Travis shook his hand, then walked back to the others as everyone left the church.

CHAPTER 7

The closer they got to the hotel, the more Travis's nervousness increased until he wanted to crawl out of his skin. Everyone who had attended their wedding party was completely taken with his new bride. He'd watched as she spoken to each person upon their arrival, making them feel at ease and welcome as if she'd been doing it for years. Stella was going to be perfect for the hotel. Her pleasant personality would, indeed, bring in paying customers and make all of his plans work out. Now he just had to figure out how to tell her their marriage was a ruse.

"Levi told me you were shot not long ago. Does it still bother you?" Stella asked.

"Not really." He cupped his palm around her elbow and assisted her up the step and onto the sidewalk in front of the hotel. In the dim light of evening, he saw a brief flash of her white teeth as she smiled at him...or the gesture, he wasn't sure which. He placed the key in the simple brass lock on the front door, but before he could turn it, the door swung open. "I thought I locked this when Levi and I left for the church?"

Hesitantly, he pushed the door open wider and heard

Stella's harsh gasp. The newly rebuilt front desk lay in pieces on the floor, the axe still lodged in a large section of the top. Ugly vomit-colored paint had been tossed all over the walls and across the floor. He closed his eyes, knowing it was only a matter of minutes, maybe seconds, until Stella started in with the questions; questions he didn't have answers for—at least not any he could readily give her that wasn't a lie. And he refused to do that to her. He couldn't abide lies, which is why Stella not knowing about their marriage was eating at him. Exaggeration maybe, leaving bits of information out, sure...but definitely no lies.

Stella walked by him, carefully avoiding the thick pools of paint as she made her way down the hallway. "Do you think they only did this to the lobby?"

"I hope so." Travis followed her to the dining room and leaned over her shoulder to survey the damage, surprised by her reaction. Maybe she wasn't like most women, and he'd sorely misjudged her?

He was glad to see that most of the tables and chairs remained intact. Only a few chairs looked like they'd been slammed against the floor. Two of the tables were missing legs, and one had a hole chopped out of its center, but nothing else in the room was damaged. "I guess they concentrated their destructive energy on the lobby."

She nodded and turned her head to look at him, but stopped. She was so close, his lips almost touched hers. She stared at his mouth, her gaze slowly rising to meet his. All he had to do was lean forward just a hair's breadth more....

The tip of her tongue peeked out, running over her bottom lip and leaving a trail of tempting moisture in its wake. The thought of what it would be like to kiss her had kept him awake for hours—and now he was close enough to find out. He shoved away the impulse and forced his feet to take a step back, away from her tempting mouth. "I'm not worried about the kitchen. They couldn't have done much to make it worse than it already was."

Stella chuckled, the pleasant sound filling the otherwise empty hall and erasing some of the foreboding and guilt weighing on him. "However, we still have to check upstairs." Her eyes suddenly widened. She pivoted, racing toward the stairwell muttering to herself. "Whoever it was better not have touched my room or they will regret messing with me." Her voice was a steady hiss as she continued to grumble, her mouth set in a rigid line as she galloped up the stairs.

Her vehemence surprised Travis as he climbed, taking two stairs at a time to keep up with her. Maybe Stella wasn't the meek and mild lady he'd thought she was.

A sudden thought made his blood run cold. What if whoever had done this was still here? When he reached the top landing, he grabbed for Stella's arm, but she was too quick. "Stella, stop!" he hissed. "Whoever did this could still be here!"

She slowed, coming to a complete stop and faced her door. Pulling the gun from the back of his waistband, he nodded, ignoring the scowl she aimed at the gun.

"Seriously? You wore a gun to our wedding?" she hissed.

He shrugged. "I'm never without my gun." He motioned with a jerk of his head toward the door. She flung the door open and took a step into the room and tripped on the braided rug. With a shrill squeak she pitched forward. Travis lunged forward, grabbing her by one shoulder and pulling her back against his chest. Her body stiffened in his grip, but he didn't release her. She trembled, and his grip tightened. A sweet floral scent filled his nostrils. He rested his cheek against the side of her head, breathing her in. Before he was ready, he raised his head.

Her bedroom had been destroyed. Someone had torn apart her trunk; ripped bodices and skirts were strewn across the floor. Tufts of cotton spewed out from large slices in the mattress, and the quilt was nothing more than shreds of material. "Stella, I'm sorry. Tomorrow, we'll go to Ida and John's store and replace everything." She let out a loud sigh and finally relaxed, her body pressing against his. He dropped his arms and quickly stepped back, almost making her fall again...but he didn't want her to feel how his body responded to hers.

Stumbling backward, she waved her arms in a frantic motion to balance herself. He raised his hand, not quite touching her back, just in case she needed his help. He bit back a groan. She must think him a klutzy oaf—but better that than letting her think he was amorous. "I'm sorry.... We need to talk," he blurted as he ran his fingers through his hair then smoothed down his mustache, trying to figure out what to say to her. A repetitive tapping pulled at his attention, and he realized Stella now stood with her arms crossed over her very nice chest, one small foot tapping out a staccato rhythm against the floor.

"Well? Am I supposed to stand here and wait all night or are you going to spit out what you wanted to say?" She continued to glare at him. "If it's about you being a gambler, I already know. Not that I approve—I don't—but that's neither here nor there."

His eyes widened. He bit back a smile at her sharp wit. It gave him another glimpse into her ever-changing character. Unfortunately, it didn't diminish his opinion of her. In fact, it added to it, which was a distraction he didn't need. It would have been much easier for him to keep his distance if she wasn't beautiful or likable. He cleared his throat. "I know this should have been said before we married, but with everything that's happened...." She stood a bit straighter. "I'm afraid I've unintentionally brought you into something...well, something untoward. I'm sorry for that. I'd hoped after winning this place to make it successful before selling it, and I needed your help."

She frowned. "Like a business arrangement?"

"Exactly. I never planned on marrying. I don't stay in one town long enough to settle down." He let out a breath of frustration. "What I mean to say is I never planned for our union to be anything but platonic, so you don't have to worry about that."

She nodded, her lips turning white as they pressed together. Her stomach tightened into a painful knot, and her muscles tensed as she held back her anger. "If that's what you want," she bit out. Needing to change the subject until she had a chance to mull over what she'd just heard—as well as stopping herself from saying something she'd regret—she asked, "Now I have a question for you...why do you gamble?"

He didn't know how she found out about his chosen profession this fast, and he wasn't quite sure how to answer her. "It's a means to an end, I guess? Never was much good at anything else."

"Well, now I understand why you asked for a wife with hotel experience in your letter." Her gaze moved around the room, and he saw the slight trembling of her chin. "If you don't mind, I would like to retire for the evening. Today has been quite taxing, and I still have to straighten my room."

He stepped out into the hallway. As she moved to close her door, he rested his palm against the warm wood. "I promise to get to the bottom of this as quickly as possible. I'll stop whoever's doing this." He met her sad gaze and dropped his hand. "I am truly sorry—for everything."

Just before the door closed, he heard her whisper, "Good night, Travis."

He stood, staring at her door, his stomach in tight knots. He rubbed his knuckles against a spot on his chest. He'd made a terrible mistake. He should have talked to a few married men before jumping the gun and writing that letter.

He closed the door to his room behind him and sat on the edge of his bed, uncaring that most of the mattress stuffing was scattered on the floor around him. It was too late now, and he would just have to make the best of it. Thankfully, once the hotel was fixed, again, he could spend his days at the saloon as usual and avoid any future confrontations with his new wife. At least that's what he hoped would happen.

STELLA COULDN'T MOVE. Her heart hurt, her pride hurt, and her head hurt. Closing her eyes, she rubbed her temples, willing the carnage of her belongings to disappear. She knew it wouldn't, though. She took several deep breaths then opened her eyes again, forcing her legs to move her toward the bed. Dropping onto the edge of the cut up mattress, she stared at the remains of her wardrobe scattered across the floor. She leaned over and picked up what had been her favorite yellow skirt. Smoothing the material, she noticed three long slashes down the center of the skirt, the edges clean as if cut with scissors or a knife.

She laid the garment across her bed, a sudden urge to fix something propelling her across the room to her trunk. Digging through the few cherished books at the bottom, she found the small sewing kit her grandmother had given her as a child and the nightgown and peignoir her parents had given her as a wedding present. Carrying the items to the bed, she quickly inspected them and found no damage. She let out a sigh of relief. Taking off her wedding dress, she slipped into the nightgown, then opened up the sewing kit.

She sat on the end of her bed and turned the skirt inside out, pressing the slits together and pinning them. Threading a needle, she sewed the damaged sections back together. She flipped the skirt right side out and held it up. A sense of satisfaction bubbled up through her previous dismay. The damage was barely noticeable.

Going through the rest of her clothes took several more hours, but when she was done repairing what she could, she'd been able to salvage two more skirts and three blouses. She folded the rest of the ruined items and placed them back into the trunk, then turned toward the bed, exhausted.

She scowled at the damaged mattress and shredded bedcovers. They hadn't even left the pillow untouched. She thought about the other rooms, wondering if they'd also been ransacked. If she was going to get any sleep tonight, she would have to look.

With a sigh, she shrugged on the matching peignoir, tying the ribbon at her neck into a bow. She cracked open the door wide enough to see across the hall, making sure Travis's door was closed. She opened the door a bit more and slipped through, praying the hinges wouldn't squeak and give her away. When they didn't, she tiptoed to the room next to hers and looked inside. Her heart fell. The damage to the bed in that room was even worse.

Tiptoeing to the room Levi had pointed out to her earlier as his, she peeked inside and smiled. Levi was sleeping on his mattress despite the damage done to his room. She quietly closed his door then checked the rest of the rooms. None had been spared. The mattresses were all cut open, the sheets and beautiful quilts destroyed. She hated to admit it, but her bed was in the best condition.

No longer tired, she walked down the staircase and sat on the bottom riser. What was she going to do now? Nothing had gone as she'd planned. This wasn't the life she'd dreamed about. The train ride to this deplorable town hadn't been the exciting adventure she'd hoped for. Her trousseau had been stolen. Evidently not once, but twice now, the hotel had been vandalized. And the worst part, her marriage was nothing more than a farce.

Leaning her shoulder and head against the railing, she twined her fingers together in her lap and stared in front of her, not really seeing anything as she considered her options…if she even had any. She still had the money her father had given her for a return ticket to Chattanooga, should she need it. But did she really want to go back home?

Travis had lied to her. She'd been so naïve; she knew that now. To her, advertising for a bride meant that a husband wanted a wife—in the truest sense of the word. Someone to make a home with, eventually have children with. There were evidently more reasons for wanting a bride, and her new husband's reason seemed to be his need for a hotel manager. She let out a loud sigh and closed her eyes, too tired to care but not tired enough to sleep. She didn't have a decent bed to sleep on anyway.

"Couldn't sleep either?"

Startled, she wrapped one hand around her throat. Jumping away from the stairs, she whirled around, wide-eyed. Seeing Travis, she dropped her hand with a quick scowl. "Don't do that! You scared me half to death!"

He burst out laughing and dropped onto his own step, his hands hanging over his knees. "I'm sorry...but I didn't think eyes could open quite that much."

He continued chuckling under his breath as she glared at him, her heart fluttering—not from fear this time, but at how handsome he was. Vexed with herself, she propped her fists against her hips. "My brothers found out very quickly—I do *not* like being snuck up on. Don't do it again."

His mouth twisted to one side, giving him a childish, mischievous look. "Or what? If you're going to threaten someone, you'd better make it good or they'll just ignore you and do it again anyway."

Her scowl deepened, and she stomped her foot with a growl. "Oh! You are impossible! First you lie to me, and now you're telling me what I should and shouldn't do!"

He held up one hand, his smirk gone. "Wait a minute. I never lied to you—about anything. I just didn't get a chance to talk to you before we got married."

She crossed her arms over her chest, one finger tapping against her elbow. "It was a lie of omission, which is the same thing. You could have taken five minutes to explain things, but instead, you didn't give me the chance. What if I didn't want a marriage like that? Maybe I expected a marriage of love?"

One eyebrow rose. "Did you?"

She looked away, her anger fizzling to a low simmer. "Well, not immediately, but eventually…yes, I did expect a marriage of love. But that's beside the point. Just because a few bad things happened, it doesn't excuse what you did." She paced around the piles of broken wood and wildly flung her arms around her. "Is this what I have to look forward to for the rest of my life? I left a beautiful town with evergreens, lakes, and mountains everywhere, not to mention my family. I will miss my brothers growing into men, and I won't be able to help my parents as they grow older either. I left all of that because I thought you wanted me as your wife! What choice have you given me? I get to manage your hotel. Will I even earn my own wages? Do I have to answer to you like a boss?"

Her shoulders sagged, but she just stood there as if her feet had sprouted roots into the floor. All of her energy had dissipated with her short rant. She breathed deep, letting the breath out in a slow hiss. "I am sorry. You didn't deserve...well, you did, but not like that. I shouldn't have yelled at you."

Head canted, he narrowed his eyes. "You intrigue me,

Stella McCord...Stone. I had every intention of telling you my plans. If you think I kept them from you on purpose, I am truly sorry. Yes, I'm a gambler, and this...." he said as he threw a glance around the lobby, "...is new to me. I've never had anything of my own before. I'll admit, it isn't starting out well, but I have faith that you know what you're doing. I have faith in you. If you'll give me a chance, I would like to work together to make this hotel a success."

He got up and moved to stand in front of her, picking up her hands and holding them in his. "I *need* this hotel to work. I made a promise to you today, and I mean to keep it for as long as I can. But if what you want is a love match, I'm afraid I can't give you that. I can't be a true husband. I'm sorry. I've been alone for a very long time, and don't have a clue what a family is like. You'll need to have patience until I get the hang of what we have now, but I'm willing to try if you are?"

Stella swallowed, not quite sure what to make of the flash of emotion in his eyes when he said he wouldn't even try to become a real family. The moment her hands touched his, a tiny *zing* raced through her. She liked his touch, liked the way the newly formed callouses at the base of his fingers felt against her skin. They weren't work-roughened yet, but after renovating the hotel, his touch wouldn't be quite so soft. She liked that thought.

Her mind raced as she realized she had lied to him too, and that knowledge wasn't sitting well as her stomach churned uncomfortably. She'd worked the front desk in her father's hotel, but had never been in charge of the day-to-day goings on. The situation she found herself in now was a bit more entailed than just checking people into rooms. Could she do it?

She straightened her shoulders, refusing to give in to doubts now when she never had before. This was one situation where she was going to put her stubbornness to good use and succeed. No one in Carlsbad knew her. If she was careful, and kept her actions and mouth in check, she just might come out of this with everything she wanted—respectability, and a good job where she could help people. She couldn't deny her reaction to Travis, both physical and emotional. If she played her cards right, maybe she'd get her husband to realize he needed her…not just as a hotel manager, but as a real wife.

Staring into Travis's blue gaze, she wanted to find out more about this man. She was drawn to him. Whether he liked it or not, somehow she would figure out how to make this marriage work. Not his version, of course. She wanted to love and be loved. More than anything else, she desired the heartfelt emotion clearly evident in her parent's eyes whenever they looked at each other. Somehow, she'd figure out how to make Travis Stone change his mind about her and their marriage.

CHAPTER 8

When he heard the sound of boots on the sidewalk in front of the hotel, Travis glanced up from what he was doing. Two seconds later, Tom and Ben walked into the lobby. He carefully placed the hammer over the top of the nail bucket beside him and wiped his sweaty palms against his jeans before bracing his arms, hands outstretched, on the new desktop.

He bit back a laugh at the incredulous looks crossing their faces, quickly morphing into scowls as they took in the new damage. "Morning Ben, Sheriff."

"What the hell, Stone?" Tom said.

Ben shook his head. "Damn, man. If you didn't like our efforts, you should've said something before we spent all day workin' to help you get this place ready for the missus."

Travis chuckled. "Had an unknown visitor while we were all at the wedding. Guess whoever it was didn't like what any of us did." He glanced at the sheriff. "Levi delivered my message, I assume? Figured you'd want to know about the newest break-in."

Tom rested his hands on top of the two pistols he wore

low on his hips. "Stop with the 'sheriff' business. We worked side by side for days fixing this place up. Call me by my given name. And yes, Levi gave me your message, albeit an abbreviated version. All he said was you wanted us to come over here." His gaze moved around the room again. "Any ideas who might have done this?"

Travis shrugged. "Guess I need to explain to the kid the importance of information. I have a few ideas, but nothing concrete. You were at the table, or at least close enough to hear the threats. What do you think?"

The sheriff scrubbed his lower face with his hand, a habit much like Travis's when he was troubled or thinking about something. "Jacob Smithton and Will Cathcart both threatened you. There's that British gent too. He seemed riled up as well. You play a mean hand of poker. Hell, within one day of you being here, everyone in town knew to steer clear of your table."

"Cards are natural to me, always have been. Learned to play when I was young, and took to it like cacti to the desert. Can't help it if people lose, especially if they wager items important to them. Stupid, if you ask me."

"What's stupid?" Stella asked, walking into the room.

The men turned to her. Tom and Ben pulled off their hats and nodded. "Ma'am," they said in unison.

"Would either of you like a cup of coffee or tea? I even have fresh-squeezed lemonade."

In a well-practiced motion, they lifted their hats back to their heads, settling them in place with a tip and pull. Ben smiled with a wink. "I never turn down an offer of lemonade, Mrs. Stone."

Stella laughed, the light, airy sound somehow lifting the oppressive feeling hanging in the air. "Call me Stella, both of you." She glanced first at Tom then Travis. "And you two?"

"Lemonade for me," Travis said.

"Me too, if you don't mind," Tom answered.

"I don't mind at all, Sheriff."

"Tom. No one here is a stranger."

"Thank you...Tom. Be back in two shakes with your drinks." Stella headed back to the kitchen where she'd been working trying to straighten up the mess in there, what little there had been. Now Travis knew what had been taking her so long to finish up.

"She seems to be settling in well," Tom said. "Even with whatever it is you've started."

"Me?" Travis frowned. "I didn't start this. Best you get that in your thick head. I played an honest game of cards and won fair and square."

Tom raised his hand. "I wasn't insinuating anything. But you have to admit your problems started when you won this hotel."

Travis bit back another strong retort and chewed on the inside of his cheek. Tom had a point—one he definitely couldn't argue against—and the addition of Stella just added to his problems. "Jacob Stockton threatened me when he lost the hotel, and a couple more times before the game you happened to step in on. Will Cathcart didn't seem too pleased either."

"No, he didn't at that. As the younger brother, Silas follows Will's lead, so you'd better be on the lookout for both of them. That Englishman left town later that same day, so he's off the list." Tom pulled out the stump of a cigar from his pocket and stuck it between his lips, chewing on the end.

"Why don't you buy yourself a new cigar? The store has plenty of them, you know," Travis asked.

"My wife would have my head on a platter. She wants me to quit—doesn't like me smelling of tobacco all the time."

Ben chuckled. "Bernice is a gem. Sweetest woman you've ever seen until she gets a bee in her bonnet. The only advice I can give you is to run as fast as you can in the opposite direction."

Tom nodded, a pleased look on his face. "That's my Bernie all right."

"Here we are," Stella announced, setting an oblong, tarnished silver tray on the desktop. Picking up two of the glasses, she handed them to Tom and Ben, the third she gave to Travis. Wiping her palms on her apron, she leaned against the end of the front desk and crossed her arms over her chest, which Travis had a hard time not staring at.

"Now, gentlemen, who's going to explain the situation to me?" Stella glared at each of them. "And I want the truth. Whether you like it or not, I'm now a part of whatever's happening, and I deserve the right to know what I'm up against." When no one spoke, she moved a step closer to Travis and tapped her foot on the floor and raised her brows. "Travis?"

He didn't know what to tell her that wouldn't have her running out the door as fast as she could back to Chattanooga. Whether he liked it or not, he did need her help. He hadn't resented her presence as much as he'd thought he would. Much to his surprise, he rather liked it—and her. He knew he was going to have to come clean with her. He hadn't been entirely truthful with her, and that fact wasn't setting well with him. His mother had always told him that a man without his word didn't have anything.

"I'm not going to ask again. One of you better start talking."

Ben choked on his lemonade. "Guess Bernice isn't the only one who can dress a fellow down."

Tom shook his head with a smile. "No, Ben, I reckon she's not. Not anymore." He gulped the rest of his drink and set the glass back on the tray. "That was delicious, ma'am. Thank you."

"As you just pointed out, Tom, we aren't strangers anymore. Please call me Stella." She gave Ben a pointed stare as well. "You too…Ben."

Ben's lips twitched, and he gave her a nod. Setting his empty glass beside Tom's, he followed the sheriff to the door, his limp barely noticeable this morning. With his hand gripping the doorknob, he tipped his hat with a slight nod. "Thank you, Miss Stella. The lemonade was indeed delicious." He gave Travis a knowing grin. "Seems like you've got some explainin' to do." He closed the door behind him, his laughter following him down the street.

Before Travis could open his mouth, the front door opened again. Levi stepped into the room carrying a covered dish in his hands, a scowl on his face.

Travis rose to his full height as the boy handed the dish to Stella. "Levi, what's wrong?"

Levi shook his head with a sigh and gave a furtive glance toward Stella. Her gaze narrowed.

"It's okay, I was going to tell her anyway. Now that she's here, she should know too," Travis said.

Levi shrugged his shoulder. "Heard a couple of rumors, and now people are startin' to talk."

"What kind of rumors?" Travis asked.

"I've only heard two so far. One is that you stole the hotel from Stockton." Travis snorted, dismissing it immediately, and nodded for Levi to continue. "Well…." The boy fidgeted then stuffed his hands inside his front pockets. "I was walkin' by the Two Johns—"

"What's the Two Johns?" Stella interrupted.

"A saloon. Anyway, I was walking' by the Two Johns and heard several of the men talkin' about how good you are at cards. They said you were too good. One of them even suggested you might be on the run from the law. Another Doc Holliday."

Stella glanced between them, her brow raised. "Wasn't Doc Holliday one of the good guys?"

"Depends on who you talk to," Travis answered. "Very few men could rival him at cards, and he was a deadly shot. Proved that when he helped Wyatt Earp round up the Cowboys. Most old timers considered him the most dangerous man in the West. I play poker, and I can shoot straight, but I'm nowhere near what Holliday was." He downed the lemonade and set his glass on the tray, which Stella promptly picked up.

She glanced at Levi. "Would you like some lemonade too? The men seemed to think it was good."

"I sure would, Miss Stella. It's a scorcher out today!"

"Go on then," Travis said. "Get your drink, then help Stella finish the kitchen. Afterward, you can help me fix the broken tables and make a few new chairs. How does that sound?"

Levi gave him a nod and turned to jog after Stella as she headed toward the kitchen. "Sounds good to me!"

Travis's gaze fell to his hand, the knuckles white from gripping the hammer so tight. The last thing he needed was for someone to start getting suspicious and asking too many questions. During the last two weeks, he'd caught a glimpse of two or three men he knew from his past and managed to steer clear of them, but he couldn't be certain they hadn't already seen him. He'd worked hard putting his past life on the Outlaw Trail behind him. To have it unravel now, just when good things were falling into place....

He forced his hand to relax, then picked up the hammer and finished pounding in the last few nails, securing the desktop to its base. A good sanding then two coats of lacquer, and it would look even better than the first one he'd made. He'd have to thank whoever had chopped it up because they'd done him a favor. He ran his palm over the wooden top, liking the feel of the rough surface. Maybe he'd found something he could do better than winning at cards. Something respectable.

STELLA THOUGHT about what she'd just learned as she scrubbed down the walls of the kitchen. Stepping back, she looked over her progress and liked what she saw. The walls were almost an off-white, with just the barest hint of gray stubbornly clinging to the paint. The floor had also been scrubbed several times, and looked much better as well. It would definitely need a coat or two of stain to cover a couple darkened areas where liquid had spilled and soaked into the wood, however. She'd had the back door open since early that morning, airing out the staleness, which had helped more than anything else to change the room's pitiful state.

Hearing a footfall behind her, she turned to find Levi standing in the back doorway where he'd thrown away the remnants of two more chairs from the dining room. "What do you think?"

His brown gaze roamed the small room. "Smells and looks a lot better—better than when we cleaned it before you got here. Still don't look like a kitchen though. Are you sure I can't help? Travis told me to help you in here, not the dining room."

"Doesn't."

He scowled. "Huh?"

"It still *doesn't* look like a kitchen, not *don't* look like a kitchen. This room isn't big enough for two people. Levi, what grade are you in? In school?"

He shrugged. "Haven't gone to school."

Stella's eyes widened. "Never?"

"My ma taught me at home cuz we lived too far from town. I learned a lot from her before...before she died."

"I'm sorry, Levi. I didn't know. I loved attending school when I was your age. My teacher taught about the wars in Europe, how the United States was settled. My favorite was learning about ancient Egypt. I didn't care much for math, though. Nor science. Oh, it was interesting—especially some of the experiments we got to do—but when I almost blew up the building, I wasn't allowed to do them anymore."

He barked out a laugh, which completely erased the sadness in his eyes. "You almost blew up the school? Really?"

She nodded. "I'm afraid so. If you ask my father, he'd tell you I was confined to my room almost my entire childhood for things I managed to do, except for one particular event when I was six. My parents were so relieved I was okay, they forgot to punish me."

Levi sat on the clean floor and crossed his legs in front of him. "What happened when you were six?"

She glanced through the door and saw Travis still working on the front desk. "All right," she said, sitting on the floor facing him. "But this stays between you and me. Agreed?" Levi's tousled hair bobbed up and down on his head as he nodded.

"My older brother Alex and I were walking home after school. I was supposed to keep up, but I saw a pretty cat crawl into a house that had been damaged by a flood several years before.

"I'd remembered my father talking about how those houses were so badly damaged, the city needed to tear them down before something bad happened. Well, I imagined the worst and couldn't let anything like that happen to that poor cat, so I followed the cat through a broken basement window to rescue it. Unfortunately, I wasn't fast enough."

"Why?" he asked his eyes wide. "What happened?"

"Well, I heard the cat mewling in the back area and ran toward it. The house let out a loud creaking noise, then everything started falling on top of me. I pressed myself against the back wall, hoping the cat was all right, and waited for everything to stop falling. There was so much dust in the air that it was really hard to breathe. I waited for what seemed like forever until my mother found me, but then the floor above caved in some more, and a large piece of wood hit her in the head and knocked her unconscious."

She leaned forward and lowered her voice, as if telling him a secret. "I've never been so scared in my life. You see, my real mother left me and my father, and I was angry at everyone and everything. My stepmother, Lucie, helped me stop being so angry. But because I'd disobeyed, I thought I'd killed her. Not surprisingly, my father showed up and got us both out before the house completely collapsed. My stepmother was fine, of course, but it took me a while to forgive myself."

She wrapped her hands around Levi's, which were gripping his legs. "What I learned was that life is full of unexpected miracles. You just have to pay attention so they don't pass you by."

Levi slowly nodded, a thoughtful expression on his face. "You're right, Miss Stella. Life *is* full of surprises. I thought I was going to be alone forever until I found Travis. He makes sure I eat every day, and even bought me clothes. He reminds me a lot of my pa."

She squeezed his hands, then let go and stood up. "Then I'm very glad you found him. I know I don't know Travis very well yet, but my intuition tells me you're right. Travis Stone is a very good man. Now, didn't I hear something mentioned about you helping him build some chairs?"

Levi smiled and nodded, his hair flopping on his forehead. He absently brushed the locks away with his fingers, much like she'd seen Travis do when he was annoyed. He hopped up, and before she could blink he ran from the room, his boots clomping down the hall toward the lobby.

She walked to the back door and stepped outside, the hot air searing her skin as she walked across the sunbaked ground. She really missed the lush greenery she'd grown up with. She wasn't yet accustomed to the heat in New Mexico, and wasn't sure she ever would be.

Growing up, her favorite time of day had been sitting on the front porch, watching the cool, early morning mist bubble like water running over rocks in a stream as it blanketed the ground. She stared at the surrounding desert, so dry and arid. Heat shimmered everywhere she looked, and all she smelled was dirt baking in the high heat. What she wouldn't give to smell the heavy scent of her mother's roses that grew around the porch back home, or the fragrance of the evergreen trees after a spring rain.

Sighing, she turned and raised her hand to her forehead, shading her eyes as she stared at the back wall of the hotel. No wonder the kitchen had seemed odd from the inside. It looked like whoever had built the hotel added the room as an afterthought. The three walls and flat roof stuck out from the back of the hotel like a giant wart. An idea popped into her mind, and she ran inside and up the stairs to her room where she pulled out a single piece of her stationery and a pencil.

Kneeling beside her trunk, she used the flat top as a table and drew out a floor plan based on her idea. After a few changes, she sat back and stared at the drawing, pleased with what she saw. Instead of the small and unusable kitchen jutting away from the hotel like it was now, she'd expanded the floor space by moving the perpendicular wall adjoined to the dining room until it was the same length. She'd moved the back wall of the kitchen, adding another three feet so there would be enough room to move around and actually cook. The third wall she moved back about two feet, overlapping the back of the hotel where the office was. It was now the perfect space for a good-sized pantry, which every hotel kitchen needed.

Carrying her handmade design downstairs, she stopped on the bottom riser and looked around the lobby, her gaze resting on the check-in desk. Her new husband was definitely talented with wood. The front desk was every bit as beautiful as the one in her father's hotel in Chattanooga. The floor had been sanded and stained again, the darker color looking more elegant. He'd even painted the walls a light yellow, which made the area bright and inviting. She couldn't wait to begin decorating, adding a few perfect items that would make people staying there feel welcome. Her grandmother had always told her that simplistic beauty was what people wanted—to feel relaxed and comfortable in a place that wasn't home—and she intended to carry on that tradition.

She heard Travis's low voice coming from the dining room, followed by the pounding of his hammer. Evidently, he'd begun fixing the broken furniture. Glancing down at her drawing, she took a deep breath and moved toward the loud ruckus coming from the dining room. It was now or never. After all, she thought, the worst that could happen would be for him to say no. Quietly, she stood in the doorway watching as Travis showed Levi how to fix a chair leg. The eleven-year-old followed the instructions to the letter. From where she stood, it actually looked as if he did a good job.

Travis raised his head as if he could feel her gaze on him, and his blue gaze met hers. She was struck again at how handsome he was, and her stomach fluttered like a hundred butterflies were trying to escape. "Do you have a moment?" She cleared her throat, not liking the breathiness of her voice. "I'd like to show you something—plans."

One brow rose. "What kind of plans?" When she didn't

answer, he pulled his watch out of his vest pocket. "Why don't we call it a day?" He smiled at Levi. "Want to run over to the restaurant and pick up supper? Mabel sent over one of her cobblers earlier, so we already have dessert."

Levi jumped up. "Sure I will! Do I put it on your tab?"

"Yep."

Stella stepped into the room as Levi barreled past her. Her smile widened when she heard the front door open and close with quiet *snicks*. He constantly amazed her with his thoughtfulness and care of both people and things. Most boys wouldn't have given it a thought, and slammed the door as they ran out. Not Levi.

Travis stood and wiped his hands with a dirty rag, then pulled a chair out and waited behind it as she walked toward the table. Sitting, he pushed her closer to the table and grabbed a chair of his own. "Now, show me what's got you so excited."

She frowned and sat back. "What makes you think I'm excited?"

His lips twitched. "Your eyes sparkle, and your whole face lights up."

Her cheeks warmed under his continued perusal. Flustered, she laid the piece of paper on the table between them and pushed it closer to him. "I drew up plans for making the kitchen better." She waited with baited breath when Travis picked up the paper and seemed to study it. Her lungs screaming, she let the trapped air out and continued to wait, growing increasingly impatient the longer he took.

"I think we can do this." Travis's low voice startled her in the soundless room.

"Really? You like it?"

He laid the plans flat on the tabletop, his head canted to one side as he stared at her. "I do. You've thought of everything we would need to make it a usable kitchen. A kitchen worthy of this hotel. Thank you, Stella."

She wanted to do a jig but remained seated, basking in his praise. He seemed genuinely pleased with her idea, and the way he looked at her, almost hungry, definitely didn't feel platonic. It took everything she had, but she kept her face normal, as if nothing between them was changing. Maybe, just maybe, there was still hope for her future…not as a hotel manager, but as Travis's wife.

CHAPTER 9

Stella opened her eyes as the morning sun peeked over the sandy horizon. Her gaze was drawn to the window where the hillside beyond basked in the golden glow. As she watched, the desert came to life, and the line demarcating night from day faded as the sun rose in the sky.

She stretched, loving the feeling of her sore muscles. Something else to add to her growing list of new things she'd experienced since her arrival in Carlsbad almost three weeks ago. Much to her surprise, she had grown quite fond of the quiet desert town. The people here were every bit as nice as back home, and she didn't miss her family quite as much as she had the first two weeks. Since their grand reopening the previous weekend, her job managing the hotel kept her busy as people began to check in.

Quickly dressing, she splashed cold water on her face and braided her hair, twisting the long tress into a tight bun on top of her head. Looking at her reflection in the mirror, she lightly pinched her cheeks to bring a bit of color into her pale complexion, then went downstairs for her morning oatmeal before guests began arriving for their own breakfast. The idea of providing a good breakfast to the guests free of charge had been her own, and everyone seemed to both like and appreciate the novel approach. It held them apart from the other hotels in town, and their occupancy had more than doubled in just six days.

While the guests were eating, she ran back upstairs and changed out the dirty bed sheets for clean in the newly vacated rooms, which took longer than she liked. But with Levi manning the front desk downstairs, she got everything done without any interruptions.

With her hands full of dirty linen, she was halfway down the staircase when she heard an unfamiliar male voice in the lobby. The angry drawl unnerved her. She moved down another step, but something about the man's stance, as if he were about to pounce, made her stop. Or maybe it was the way his hand fondled the butt of the gun he wore low on his hip.

Levi's expression was blank. He seemed safe enough for now, so she continued to listen to what the disgruntled man was saying.

"You're sure you don't know more about Travis Stone than you're tellin' me? Like where he comes from...what he did before? If you ask me, he seems to be mighty secretive. Only people with something to hide keep secrets. I used to know someone like him—and believe me, he wasn't a nice person at all. He used to ride the Outlaw Trail with some of the most dangerous men alive."

Levi shook his head and let out a loud sigh. "Sir, I've told you everything I know. Mr. Stone is a good, hard-working man. I've seen it myself—he's been working from sunup to sundown getting this here hotel fixed and ready."

"What about this supposed wife of his?"

She hurried down the stairs and walked up behind him. "I'm Mrs. Stone. What can I do for you, sir?"

The man whirled around with a scowl on his face. His gaze moved up and down her body until she wanted to slap his face to the back of his head. At least then he wouldn't be looking at her anymore.

"So you're the painted lady Travis shacked up with?"

Levi's expression morphed from indifference to an angry scowl, and he braced his arms against the desktop. "Don't you dare say anything bad against Mrs. Stone. She's a wonderful lady. I'll not sit here listening to any more of your lies, so you can leave!"

Her eyes widened at the man's vulgarity, and before she realized what she was doing, she squeezed her hand together in a tight fist, pulled back her arm, and hit him in the nose. Blood splattered across his face as he pinched his nose between his fingers with a howl. She took a step back as the man mumbled something unintelligible under his breath then stalked out of the hotel. Stella couldn't have wiped the smile from her face if she'd tried. Hitting someone had never felt so good.

Shaking out her hand, she turned to Levi, a giggle escaping when she saw his open-mouthed expression as he stared back at her. Never before had anyone defended her in such a chivalrous manner, and her heart swelled with pride at Levi's reaction. Somehow, over the last three weeks, he'd wriggled his way firmly into her heart. She picked up the bed sheets that had fallen to the floor and stuffed them back into the basket. Readjusting the basket against her hip, she gave him a quick wink. She walked toward the back of the hotel and the covered porch Travis had added so she could do the washing without looking like a lobster when she was finished.

She couldn't keep her mind on her job though; her

thoughts kept returning to the rude man's insinuations about her husband's past. She hated to admit she'd long had her own misgivings about his life since she met him, and the stranger's questions only made her curiosity stronger. Why was Travis so evasive about it? Every time she asked a question, he changed the subject. At first, she'd thought it was simply because he was reserved and would open up once he got to know her better. As of yet, that hadn't happened. In fact, when Travis was around, he hardly talked to her at all. Oh, he'd ask the expected questions, such as how her day had gone and if Levi was helping, but it was never anything more than mundane conversation. And it was infuriating.

She hung the last sheet on the line to dry, then grabbed the basket and went back inside. She still had an hour or so before she needed to start supper, so she poured herself and Levi a glass of lemonade each and carried them to the lobby. "Thirsty?" She handed him a glass, shaking her head as he gulped it down.

"Can I go get another? Please?"

She chuckled. "Yes, you may—but without running." He jerked to a slow walk and continued toward the kitchen without a backward glance. She shook her head and moved in front of the check-in desk. Standing at the window, she stared out into the dusty street. Several buildings had been constructed across from the hotel: a doctor's office with an adjoining drugstore, a laundry owned by two Chinamen, and another livery a bit further down…which Ben hadn't been too happy about, since his livery had been the only one on this end of town. Now he had to fight for business, which kept him busy. Other than people getting off the train, there still wasn't much traffic at this end of town yet. The street remained empty most days.

A dark shape moved under the shadowed boardwalk of the doctor's office, and she watched the rude stranger step out into the bright sunlight. His nose was swollen, but it looked like he'd cleaned up the blood. Too incensed before, she studied him now. He was of average height and build with the kind of face that disappeared into a crowd—well, other than the huge nose. With his dirty hat pulled low over his face, she couldn't tell what color his hair was, and couldn't remember noticing before. From a distance, his dark eyes were penetrating, making her feel like he could reach inside her head and see her thoughts. She shivered but held her ground, unwilling to give him the satisfaction of knowing how uncomfortable he made her.

He reached up and touched the brim of his hat, then turned and walked around to the backside of the doctor's office. She really didn't like knowing he was watching the hotel, and her suspicions increased regarding the man's motives. Could he be mistaking Travis for someone else?

"Stella? Is something wrong?"

She jumped, and whirled around to find Tom staring at her with a worried expression on his face, holding his dusty hat in his hand. She let out a shaky laugh. "Sorry, you just startled me. I guess I was deep in thought and didn't hear you come in."

"Sorry, came in the back door." He moved a step closer, his eyes narrowing thoughtfully as he studied her. "And don't try to lie your way out of whatever is bothering you, cuz it won't work with me. I saw the look on your face as you stared out that window. Something's wrong, and I want to know what it is."

She shrugged and set her glass down on the desktop beside her. "Truthfully, I'm not quite sure. A little while ago, I came downstairs to do the laundry and overheard a man questioning Levi about Travis."

Tom frowned. "What kind of questions?"

"He asked about his past—where he came from, and if

he'd done anything other than gamble. He mentioned Travis being secretive, and that maybe it was because he was trying to hide his past. He also said Travis looked like someone he knew." She let out a shaky breath. "Normally, I wouldn't have given it another thought, but a moment ago, I caught him watching me from the shadows underneath the doctor's porch." She crossed her arms over her chest, one hand rubbing away the prickling sensation crawling along her skin. "I don't like him—or the fact that he's watching us."

"Now, I'm sure it's nothing…but if you'd like, I'll look into it. Find out who he is and why he's in town. Can you give me a name or description?"

She nodded, but before she could tell him, she heard the clapping of Levi's boots coming into the room behind them.

"Hiya, Sheriff Tom!" Levi said as he tucked himself behind the front desk again. Standing straight, he finger-combed his hair and placed his hands on the desktop.

"Hello, little man. Don't tell me Travis and Stella are letting you work the most important position in this hotel?"

Levi's eyes sparkled with joy as he smiled and gave the sheriff an enthusiastic nod. "They sure are!" He glanced at Stella. "And I've done a good job, too, haven't I, Miss Stella?"

"You've done a wonderful job! All of our guests have commented on how fast you check them in and out. They've also told me how helpful you are when they need something or want to go somewhere. Why, one gentleman told Travis your directions were better than any map."

Levi's face lit up, his brows rising to the top of his forehead. "A man really said that?"

She nodded and rested her hand on his arm. "He did. Travis and I are both proud of you, Levi." She wasn't prepared when his eyes filled with tears. Pretending she hadn't noticed, she pulled her hand away and met the sheriff's knowing gaze. "Tom, maybe Levi could tell you more than I could about the man. I'm afraid I wasn't really looking at him when he was here."

"Don't have much to go on, so it couldn't hurt." He moved to stand in front of the check-in desk and casually leaned his elbow on top, laying his hat beside his arm. "Heard you had a visitor a little while ago."

"Yessir. A man came in askin' questions about Travis—and Stella socked him in the nose! I've never seen anything like it before!"

Tom cocked his head toward Stella and scrubbed his hand across his lower face, his eyes narrowing thoughtfully. "She did, did she? Bet that *was* something to see."

"It sure was!"

Tom held her gaze another moment then gave Levi his full attention. "What kind of questions did he ask?"

Levi looked at Stella. She nodded, letting him know it was all right for him to tell the sheriff what he knew. He twisted his mouth to one side. "Well, he asked a lot of questions about Travis. You know, where he came from, how long he'd been gambling, if he carried a gun and what kind."

Tom frowned. "He asked what kind of gun he carried?"

Levi nodded but didn't say anything else.

"Can you tell me what he looked like, or anything that might stand out about him?"

Levi pursed his lips in thought, his finger tapping against his chin. "Well, one eye don't open all the way, and his right front tooth is chipped in half. Does that help?"

Tom leaned over and ruffled the kid's hair, then picked up his hat. "That's exactly what I needed. You'll make a good sheriff one day, little man."

"Nah. I think I'm gonna stay in the hotel business, like Travis and Stella."

Stella pinched her lips together to keep from laughing at the serious expression on Levi's face. The boy was truly adorable. She followed the sheriff onto the front boardwalk, and for the hundredth time, wished there was a roof over it to provide some shade. It might not make it any cooler, but at least the scorching sun wouldn't bake her skin. She'd become accustomed to the heat, but the intense light still bothered her a bit.

"What do you think is going on? Why would the man be asking about Travis?"

"Not sure, but something Levi said—about the stranger telling him he used to know someone like Travis—made me think. When Travis first came to town, I told him he reminded me of someone. It bothered me for quite a while, too. He seemed so familiar, but I couldn't place where I'd seen him before."

"That could just be a coincidence," Stella said, trying to squash the uneasy feeling knotting up her stomach. "Tom, has Travis ever told you about his past?"

He shook his head. "No, why?"

She hesitated, not wanting to raise his suspicions any more than they already were. The longer she thought about her own doubts, the more it bothered her, and she knew she should say something. "He hasn't said anything to me either," she whispered, staring at his gun. She forced her gaze to his. "Not one word about his childhood, his family, nothing. Why would he keep it all a secret?"

"Let me do a little digging before we both go off half-cocked. I know he's been spending most of his days at the Alamo, trying to win enough money to cover the cost of adding your kitchen. He also mentioned building a front awning. With the sun blasting through the window all day, it gets hot in there. Adding a cover will help to keep the lobby a little cooler, anyway."

Stella laughed, amazed. Travis was trying to fix everything she wanted, and it was a heady feeling. "I've been griping about that from the moment I saw the place. The front looks so ugly and flat. An awning would be perfect. And maybe I can get him to build me a few window boxes with the leftover pieces of wood."

The skin around Tom's eyes crinkled as he smiled. "Punched him in the nose, eh?"

She felt her cheeks heat, but nodded. "I didn't like how he talked to me."

Tom let out a loud guffaw and hit his hat against his leg. Still chuckling, he settled it in place on his head. "I'm glad you're here, Stella. Didn't know how boring this town was until you showed up." He stepped off the wooden sidewalk and glanced over at the doctor's office then back at her. "Don't you worry none. My eyes may be old, but they're still sharp. I'll be keepin' a closer watch on things around here."

"I'm not worried about me or Levi. I'm more worried about Travis. Everyone knows he spends most of his time at the saloon. It would be easy to find him."

"That they haven't done that very thing tells me they're wantin' to drag out whatever they're planning. Just sit tight. I'll figure it out and put a stop to it."

"Thank you...Tom."

He touched his fingers to the brim of his hat then turned and strode toward the jail on the next street over. She now took comfort in how open the town was. There was no place for strange men to hide. Stepping back inside, she pasted a smile on her face. "Since no one's checked in, how about we have something simple for supper...what do you think about griddle cakes and ham?"

"What's a griddle cake?"

Stella thought a moment, remembering the more common name for them out here. "I think you know them as flapjacks?"

He licked his lips and wiggled his brows. "Better make a lot. Travis and me can eat a dozen just between us!"

"Well, all right then. How about you help me? We can set out the bell so that if someone arrives to check in, we'll hear it in the kitchen."

"Do I gotta do any cooking? I don't know how."

Walking behind him with her hands on his shoulders, she steered him down the hall toward the kitchen. "Yes, you are. It's high time you learned how to make a few things by yourself. What would happen if you got stranded in the middle of nowhere and didn't know how to cook?" She pulled out everything they'd need and set it on the long counter. "Flapjacks are the easiest thing you can make, and they're filling so you won't leave the table already hungry again."

He slowly shook his head. "I don't know. Travis never—"

"Travis never what?" Travis asked.

She didn't know how long he'd been there, but his casual stance as he leaned against the doorframe led her to believe he'd been there long enough to hear her explanation. "Good. I'm glad you're here. Now you can explain to our boy here why he needs to know how to cook—at least a few things."

Travis chuckled. "Stella's right. A man never knows when he's gonna have to fend for himself or end up starving. Take it from me. I learned how to cook the hard way. I was stuck in the desert alone without my saddlebags. No bags, no food —not even a skillet."

Levi's eyes were as big as saucers as he listened to Travis's story. "So what did you do? What did you eat?"

Travis moved to stand beside Stella and picked up one of the eggs, cracking it gently against the rim of the bowl. He threw away the shell and added the rest of the eggs, stirring them into a golden froth. She watched as he showed Levi how to measure the ingredients, then letting the boy stir until the mixture was a lumpy batter.

"Stella, why don't you let us finish this?" Travis glanced down at Levi then back at her. "Tonight, us men are going to wait on you."

She slowly nodded, not quite believing what she was seeing. She hadn't even known Travis could cook. What else didn't she know about her husband? With her feet rooted to the floor, she continued to watch the two of them as they cooked and laughed together, both sneaking an occasional flapjack from the plate as they cooked. At that moment, she understood the feelings she'd been fighting for the last few days. She had found her home—this hotel, with Travis and Levi.

Moving on instinct, without a thought in her head, she stopped in front of Travis, who held a plate piled high with delicious smelling flapjacks in one hand. Before she could talk herself out of what she was about to do, she leaned closer, standing on her tiptoes, and pressed her lips to his. Travis's other hand cupped the back of her head and drew her against him, the warmth of his body seeping through her clothes until she felt hot enough to burst into flames.

Beside them, Levi snickered. The sound of his footsteps faded, but the tip of Travis's tongue sliding over her lips pulled her attention back to what was happening. She had no idea what she was doing, or what she even wanted to happen, but when his tongue forced her lips apart, she no longer cared.

He tasted like flapjacks and peppermint. Growing bold, she slid her tongue in his mouth, dueling with his and memorizing the inside of his mouth, as he had done with hers. Her legs wobbled, and she wrapped her arms around his waist. The evidence of his desire was pressing against her. She couldn't help but wonder what it would be like to see him without clothes—would he look as good without them as he did with them on? A low moan vibrated in her throat as he pulled away. Standing this close to him, his eyes were a brilliant blue.

He took a deep breath and stepped back, seeming to recover much faster than she was. Without a word, he placed the plate on the counter and walked out the back door, leaving her standing in the room alone.

CHAPTER 10

Travis flipped another card over in front of him, not really seeing it. Gathering them up again, he shuffled and dealt another hand, not seeing that one either. How could he have been so stupid? First for kissing Stella, and secondly for walking away?

He'd walked around town most of the evening, trying to figure out what to do. But he hadn't come up with a single idea. Instead of going back to the hotel, he'd come to the Alamo and stayed all night. The familiar surroundings were normally calming…right now, though, not so much. He'd lost to various people, and his surliness was pushing the rest away. Somehow he had to calm down. The second round of repairs had taken almost everything he'd had. Why he'd agreed to make the kitchen larger he hadn't a clue. Giving in to Stella's wishes was becoming a pattern with him. One he didn't like.

Holding the deck of cards in one hand, he took a deep gulp of warm beer. He shuffled and shuffled again, not really paying attention to anything going on around him. He couldn't keep his thoughts from Stella; wondering what she was doing, or if she was furious for how he'd left her last evening. He still hadn't told her everything either, which bothered him most of all. She deserved to know what she was up against, but the longer he stayed silent, the harder it was to tell her.

"Are you just gonna sit there staring at the cards? You can teach me how to play—without money, of course," Levi said with a hopeful grin.

"You don't need to learn how to play poker, kid. It's addicting and not something an eleven-year-old should learn."

"Aww, that's not fair. You learned when you were twelve, an' I'll be twelve in a couple of weeks."

Travis finally looked up, meeting Levi's brown gaze. "Really? Your birthday is in a couple of weeks?"

Levi nodded. "Yea, but it's no big deal—never has been. It's just another day."

"What day?"

"The fifteenth."

Out of habit, Travis dealt another hand and winced when Levi grabbed up the cards, thoroughly enjoying himself. He discarded two cards, face down, and then drew two replacement cards from the deck. "Your turn."

Travis scowled. "I thought you didn't know how to play?"

He shrugged. "I kinda do, just not very well. The more I watch what you do, the better I get."

Travis glanced at his cards and put them in order from lowest to highest. He had nothing. It was the worst hand of cards he'd had all morning. With a sigh, he pulled out three cards and discarded them face down on top of Levi's and drew three more, again placing them in order. He now had two sevens. Better than nothing. He laid his cards down. "What do you have?"

Levi's grin grew as he laid his cards on the table. The kid held a flush. "What'd I win?"

He sat back and shook his head. "You lied to me, kid. You already knew how to play poker, didn't you?"

Levi's smile disappeared. "No, sir, I didn't. I was tellin' you the truth. I've watched you—you're really good."

"Are you sure you're only eleven? You talk like you're older."

He shook his head. "Nope. Just eleven...almost twelve."

"Stone, or whatever name you're goin' by now. We need to talk, you and I."

Travis glanced at the man now standing beside the table and froze. Hoping he'd kept any emotion from showing, he raised a brow. "Why would we need to talk? I don't know you." He kept his gaze trained on the man's familiar face. Travis recognized him as one of the five men he'd played cards against almost two months ago. The man had kept his hat on that day, so Travis hadn't seen Clay Anderson's unmistakable white hair. Looking at him was like looking at a younger version of the man who'd taken him in after his father's death…except for the swollen nose and black eyes. One thing he was sure of: Anderson being here was a very bad omen.

Travis caught Levi's steady gaze and motioned with an almost imperceptible nod for him to leave. Without a word, the boy slid from his chair and was gone as silently and quietly as an Indian. With a wave of his hand, Travis motioned Anderson to the newly vacated seat. The outlaw looked around then slid into it, adjusting his guns.

"Now, what would you like to talk about?" He held out the deck of cards. "Game?"

Anderson shook his head. "Not likely. Your reputation at winning is becoming legendary."

"I doubt that, but your loss. The way I've played this morning, your odds of winning are higher than normal."

The young man leaned forward, resting his elbows against the tabletop, a heavy scowl on his face. "I know who you are, Dixon."

Travis sat back. "I'm afraid you're mistaken, sir. My name is Stone. Travis Stone. Given to me by my mother after my first breath."

"Don't lie to me, Dixon. Johnny Perl is here and pointed you out. I aim to make you pay for my daddy's death, so get ready." He jerked to a stand, the chair legs scraping loudly on the wood floor. "You're gonna die real soon, you hear?"

Travis crossed his arms over his chest, the familiar cold feeling he always got before a gunfight filling him. "Oh, I hear what you're saying, mister, but you got it all wrong. Come after me, and it's you who's going to be six feet under. Not the other way around."

Anderson backed away from the table a couple of steps. "Just think. Once you're dead, who's gonna comfort that pretty lady of yours?" He rubbed the ridge of his nose with a slight wince, then let his hand drop back to rest on the handle of his gun. "I owe her for doin' this to my face."

One side of Travis's mouth rose. "Seems to me she made an improvement. Like I said, you have mistaken me for someone else." He picked up the cards and shuffled them. "Get out of town and take whoever you mentioned earlier with you, and you'll live to see another day."

Anderson scowled, his expression making him look like a petulant child, and strode out of the saloon.

"Why is it I'm always coming in here to save your butt, Stone?" Tom's face could've been made from granite. He raised his hand, and Travis wisely shut his mouth. "Maybe you should watch your back—and your family's—instead of playing cards all day. Clay Anderson isn't one to be trifled with. He's meaner than a snake. Sheriff over at Tombstone believes he was responsible for a recent murder over that away, but can't prove anything. Yet. What's he wantin' with you?"

Travis shrugged. "He thinks I look like someone. Told you I get that a lot."

"Who does he think you look like?"

The churning sensation in his gut grew. He wanted to hit something...or someone. Damn. It had taken him five years to escape his past and now, in less than ten minutes, everything he'd created was crashing down around him. He toyed with the idea of trying to lie, but Tom was no fool. He'd see through his lies in a heartbeat. He swallowed and hoped for the best. "He said I looked like a man with the last name of Dixon. No first name, though."

Tom frowned. "Now why does that name sound so familiar?" He absently stared at the far end of the saloon, then shrugged. "It'll come to me soon enough. Now, I gotta get back to the jail. Paperwork won't wait." He turned to leave, but stopped and glanced at Travis over his shoulder. "Better buy Levi a large slice of Mabel's apple pie for running over and gettin' me. Again." He chuckled and left.

Travis scrubbed his hands over his face, wanting more than anything to saddle up his horse and ride out of town. But he couldn't. Not just yet anyway. First, he had to figure out what he was going to do with Levi and Stella. It was getting harder and harder for him to stay away from her, and after last night's kiss.... An idea popped into his head. Maybe he'd take Levi out to the Hidden Gulch, or *gostahanagunti* as the Apache called the area. It was twenty miles or so northwest of town, and far enough away from both Stella and Anderson. A day or two camping by the falls would give him enough time to figure out his next step.

His decision made, he set the cards in the middle of the

table and left the saloon, hesitating in the doorway long enough to make sure Anderson and Perl weren't waiting for him. Turning toward the livery, he strode along the wooden sidewalk, his steps light instead of the heavy clomping his boots normally made. He carefully made his way down the street and breathed a sigh of relief when he slipped into Ben's livery.

His horse let out a low, guttural nicker and shook his head over his stall gate. Travis smiled and walked over to him, scratching both sides of his prominent jaw, then running his hand down one side of the animal's neck. Reaching down, Travis scooped up a handful of oats Ben kept in small buckets beside each stall entrance and held the treat under his horse's lips, the long hairs tickling Travis's hands as the animal scooped the oats into his mouth. "Missed me, Deacon? I've been meaning to take you out for a long run, but life seems to keep interfering." He spoke softly, and scooped up another handful of oats. "You don't know how much I want to just saddle you up and ride out of town."

"Didn't you know was a coward."

Travis's hand dropped to the pistol he wore strapped to his hip. Strapping it on first thing in the morning was a habit he couldn't seem to break. Now, with Anderson and Perl in town, he was glad he hadn't.

Seeing Ben standing near the back wall, horse tack in his hands, he slowly moved his hand back underneath Deacon's neck. The horse immediately brushed his large head against Travis's, knocking his hat askew.

Ben chuckled and laid the tack down on top of a long wooden trunk. "Seems your horse has missed you. Haven't seen you down this way since before your wedding. What brings you here now?"

He gave Deacon one last pat, then walked closer to where Ben stood, leaning against the last stall, his thumbs tucked behind the front waistband of his jeans. "Not rightly sure. When I left the Alamo, I'd planned on going to the hotel. Instead, my feet brought me here."

"That's your conscience talking, then."

Travis snorted. "Doubtful. Haven't had much of a conscience to speak of since I was about Levi's age." He closed his eyes for a moment and let out a loud sigh. The familiar sounds of horse hooves scraping the floor as they moved in their stalls, the swish of their tails to keep away flies, and the soft nickers as they seemed to talk to each other calmed his nerves enough for his thoughts to clear. He raised his head and met Ben's curious gaze. "I seem to have encountered a bit of a problem."

Ben's brows rose. "Just one? Seems to me you have a few more than that swirling around you."

Travis jerked his hat off and ran his fingers through his hair then jammed the hat back on his head again, pacing the wide space between the stalls on either side of the stable. "I don't need the attitude right now, Ben. I need help figuring out what to do. I just had a very close call at the Alamo, and I'm actually thinking about leaving town for a few days."

"Slow down. Don't make any rash decisions until we've talked it over. Why don't you tell me what happened?"

Travis pulled in a long, cleansing breath. "How much did I actually tell you when I was drugged?"

With a flick of his hand, Ben motioned toward a bench shoved up against the stall wall. Travis sat, leaning back against the wall for support. Ben pulled a rickety chair from the corner. In one fluid motion, he twisted it around and sat backward, leaning his arms across the top rung of the chair's back. "Well, probably not as much as you think. You mentioned the names of a few outlaws I've heard of, something about not making you do something, and that you shot your pa."

"Well, you pretty much know everything then. After our ranch failed, my mother left when I was ten. My father's drinking got worse after that, but it wasn't great before. He was a mean drunk, and took his anger and frustration out on me. It was either let him beat me to death, or kill him. I killed him."

"Ever hear from your mother again?" Ben asked.

Travis shook his head. "After that, I ran away. Found myself on the Outlaw Trail by the time I'd turned thirteen. One of the leaders took me under his wing, taught me how to take care of the horses and to cook. Later, I graduated to being a lookout for some of their jobs, but I didn't like it. I left that life, and I didn't look back. Several years later, I found myself in Arizona. I managed to win enough gambling to take the train to Denver, but before we'd even made it across the Colorado border, the train was held up.

"I'd never ridden on one before, so I just figured something had happened to the train. But when I stepped into the front car, I found myself in the middle of a robbery, and face-to-face with the man who'd taken me in and treated me like a son. He wanted to know which car held the gold. He'd heard that there was a large shipment on the train bound for the bank in Denver. I don't know what set him off more...the fact that there was no gold, or that I was seemingly standing in his way of getting it."

"What happened? Were you able to convince him to leave peacefully?"

"Nope. When I told him the train held only passengers, he got really mad and accused me of already taking the gold. Truthfully, I had no clue what that train was hauling, I just wanted him to leave without hurting anyone. I knew when Jason got that look in his eyes to watch out, but those passengers closest to him had no clue how crazy he could get. Before I could stop him, he'd grabbed a woman carrying a newborn baby. With tears running down her face, she begged him to take whatever he wanted. I will hear her soft voice pleading for him to let her and her baby go in my nightmares until the day I die."

Travis shook his head fighting the sorrow he'd buried deep inside his heart. "I couldn't stop what he did next," he whispered. "I just wasn't fast enough to stop him."

"Killed the woman and her baby?"

"He shot her, then grabbed the child from her arms and tossed it outside. I did the only thing I could before he killed everyone inside that car. I had to shoot him. I'd always known I was faster than the other two he had with him. Killed one but only winged the third, who jumped from the train as it slowed to take a turn."

"What was his name, Travis? Jason who?"

He met Ben's steady gaze. "Jason Anderson."

Ben let out a low whistle. "I can guess then why Clay's in town. He knows you killed his father." From inside his vest, he pulled out his pipe and lit it, puffing out the light gray smoke, which hung in the air between them.

"Now tell me what else has you all worked up. Have you finally had your fill of Levi?" He narrowed his eyes, studying Travis's face until a slow smile curled his lips. "It's Miss Stella, isn't it? What has she done now? Convinced you to change something else? New furniture throughout the hotel? A professional chef? What?"

Travis wiped any emotion from his face, not liking the way his gut twisted and flipped each time he thought about Stella. He didn't want to like her, and had fought this annoying attraction from the moment he first laid eyes on her. But he did like her. He liked her a lot. In his opinion, he liked her too much. "It's nothing you need to worry yourself about, my friend. Right now, she's the least of my worries," he mumbled, mentally calling himself a liar. Stella had quickly climbed to the top of his worry list, which was his problem in a nutshell. What had happened to his plans of winning as much money as he could, then leaving town? Winning that blasted hotel was what triggered all of this—his plans and his life were spiraling out of control.

He squirmed under Ben's surly stare as the man continued to suck on his pipe. "You know, a lot of your stress would disappear if you would just let Tom in on your past—what you think you're running from. It would be better if he heard the story from you, beginning to end, instead of someone else who might be ignorant as to the reasons behind those actions."

"And how am I supposed to take care of things from a jail cell? Tom would arrest me for sure."

Ben shook his head. "I wouldn't be too certain about that. Tom Higgins is the fairest man I've ever met—and I've met a lot of people over the years. With Anderson after you, you're gonna need his help."

Travis stared at him a moment then gave a curt nod. "Fine. I'll think about it. If Anderson's anything like his father was, he'll wait for an opportune time to strike, which should give me enough time to do some planning of my own." He made his way toward the stable's open double doors when Ben called his name. He stopped and looked back.

"Just make sure you don't wait too long, you hear?"

Travis nodded again and left with a heavy heart. In the saloon, Clay had been fidgety, fondling his weapon like a boy itching to prove himself a man by making a name for himself with a gun. The kid wasn't going to wait, no matter how hard Travis tried to convince himself or Ben. He had to think of something quick.

CHAPTER 11

Stella tucked in the last corner of the bed sheet and smoothed the quilt over the rest of the bed. Fluffing the goose-down pillows, she propped them against the white metal headboard and stepped back. She liked what she saw. The pitcher sat nestled inside the bowl on top of the small table. She'd also bought new material at Ida's store, a pretty white eyelet, and sewed new curtains for each of the twenty-four rooms, which brightened them up.

With a steady stream of customers checking into the hotel, her days seemed filled with never-ending jobs, but she didn't mind. In fact, she actually liked it. That had been the worst part about working in her father's hotel—the boredom. All he'd allowed her to do was sit at the front desk for six hours a day. She'd memorized every scratch and gouge on the desktop. By the time she'd left, she'd memorized the flaws in the wood-planked floor as well.

Glancing at the sun hanging just above the rim of the hills in the distance, she realized it was later than she'd thought, and headed downstairs to get supper started. Most of the hotel's customers enjoyed the restaurant, and Mabel's desserts were becoming legendary. But there were always a few people who either didn't feel like leaving the hotel or couldn't afford the restaurant's higher prices, so she usually made a simple meal for everyone. Tonight, she planned to serve one of her favorite dishes—chicken and dumplings with carrots, and chocolate cake for dessert.

Stepping into the kitchen, she grabbed her apron from the hook by the door and tied it around her waist. She'd baked the cake earlier, and had already cooked and deboned the chicken. All she had to do now was mix up the dough and drop it by teaspoonful on top of the mixture already warming on the stovetop. Once that was done, she'd frost the cake, and supper would be ready to serve.

"Can I help?"

Stella glanced at the open doorway where Levi waited expectantly. "Well, that depends. Are you really wanting to help, or sample the food?"

He grinned. "Both."

She carried the dough-filled bowl to the stove. "Okay then. You can begin by getting the rag I left on the counter and lifting the lid off this pot for me."

"Okay." Two seconds later, Levi had the lid off and was watching her scoop out the dumpling dough. "Can I drop a few too?"

She glanced down at him, his little face turned up expectantly. "Sure. I'll hold the bowl and you can scoop the dough out." She handed him the two spoons, which he deftly moved to each hand. Using one, he scooped out a generous amount of the mixture and moved his arm over the pot. "Use the other spoon—"

"I know, Miss Stella. I was watchin' you, remember? I know exactly what to do."

She pinched her lips between her teeth as he struggled with the other spoon, trying to scoop the dough from the first spoon to the pot. It took several tries, but he finally got the hang of it and made short work of the remaining dough. She placed the lid back on the pot and added another piece of wood to the stove. Most stoves sold now used coal or gas as fuel, but she'd never gotten the hang of using them, so she'd asked Travis to buy her this one. Her father had installed a coal stove in their hotel, but both she and her mother preferred the wood-burning stove.

"Now what?" Levi asked.

"Now we make frosting so *you* can frost the cake."

His eyes widened. "Me? You're gonna let me frost the cake—what if I mess it up?"

She tilted her head and twisted her mouth, her finger tapping her chin as she tried to look thoughtful. "Well, if the frosting isn't perfect, do you think it will change the taste?"

He frowned, staring at the floor for a moment then raised his gaze to hers with a snicker. "Naw. The cake will be just as good—frosting will only make it better."

"And in my opinion, if you just so happen to get it a bit thick in places, that makes the cake perfect." She proceeded to show him how to measure the ingredients, then stir it so there weren't any lumps. Next, she took a spatula and dipped it in the center of the frosting and demonstrated how to smooth it over the bottom layer of the round cake. When he was finished, Stella grabbed him by the shoulders and pulled him to her in a hug. "That looks wonderful! You're very talented at this, Levi. Did you ever cook with your mother?"

"Mmm hmm. I was too little to help Pa in the field, so I helped her. We had a lot of fun, like you and I have, creating new meals with the little food we had. The farm didn't do so well for food, so Pa was gonna buy cattle with money he and ma had saved."

Stella felt his thin body tense then begin to shiver. She closed her eyes for a moment and kissed the top of his head.

His wild hair tickled her nose, reminding her she needed to give him a haircut soon or he'd be shaggier than a bear. "You know, sometimes when bad things happen it helps to talk about it. It can ease the pain in your heart so that the next time you think about it, it doesn't hurt as much." She held him at arm's length and raised his head with her finger curled under his chin. "When you're ready, I'll be here to listen. If that's what you want."

His eyes filled with unshed tears, and his thin lips trembled, but he nodded and reached for the chocolate cake. "I'll take this into the dining room for you so people can look forward to what they're gettin' for dessert."

She stared after him and sighed. Reaching for the potholders, she picked up the large pot of chicken and dumplings. Several of families staying overnight were already seated at the tables with expectant expressions on their faces. She smiled as she set the dinner on the side table beside the spoons and bowls. Turning to them, she smiled. "Please, help yourselves."

"Aren't you gonna eat too, Miss Stella?" Levi asked.

She shook her head. "Not just yet. I want to clean up the mess in the kitchen first. You go ahead. I shouldn't be long." She heard his boots clomping behind her. She picked up the spatula and other dirty utensils and laid them in the sink.

"I'd like to talk to you now...about my family."

Saying a silent prayer of thanks, Stella laid down the rag she'd been using to wipe the sugar and flour from the countertop and turned to face him.

Levi's chest rose and fell as he took a deep breath. "My pa left early that day. He was goin' to town to buy the cows. We'd discussed it as a family the night before. He said it would take at least two days for him to get to town, and four to get back. He left me in charge of the farm. It was my job to take care of things—make sure nothing happened to Ma." He pulled in a shuddering breath. "Pa never had a chance to buy the cows though. He stopped at the saloon for a quick drink and found himself in the middle of a fight. One of the men killed him."

"Oh, sweetie, I'm so sorry."

"Two days after we buried Pa, the meat had gotten low so I went hunting rabbits. Caught two good-sized ones, too." A wistful look passed over his face. "Bet they woulda tasted good. Anyhow, I found Ma's body in the yard, tore up somethin' terrible. The Apaches had scalped her," he said in a dead tone. "I failed. I didn't keep my promise to Pa—I didn't take care of Ma."

"Levi. You were taking care of your mother. You were out hunting food so she could eat. You couldn't have done anything to stop the Indians. In fact, your fate would probably have been much worse." She needed to change the subject, and did her best to lighten her voice and sound happier than she really was when her heart was shattering. "Thank you for telling me about your parents." Without warning, Levi wrapped his arms around her waist, his grip tight enough that she couldn't breathe. But Stella didn't care, and held him to her while her heart broke for him and what he'd gone through.

Refusing to cry, she forced a smile on her face and patted his back. She stared after him as he hurried from the room, her hand over her trembling mouth as she fought to breathe. She turned to go out back and jerked to a stop. Travis stood in the doorway, but she could barely see him through the tears. Without thinking, she raced across the room and threw herself against him, wrapping her arms around his neck and sobbing against his chest.

He pulled her close, holding her tightly against him without a word as she cried until she had no tears left. She softly hiccoughed and pulled back, wiping her palms over the large wet stain across his shirt. "I've ruined your shirt." She hiccoughed again.

"It's only water; it'll dry." He cleared his throat and wiped the tears from her cheeks with his thumbs. "Thank you. No one's been able to break through the wall he'd built around his heart, and I've been worried he'd stay that way."

He continued to softly rub her cheek, the back of his hand rough and wonderful. Stella didn't want to break the spell, so she kept quiet, occasionally letting out a soft sniff—not that it was a total lie, because her nose ran something awful when she cried. Before she realized he'd stopped stroking her skin, he cradled her face between his palms and slowly drew her closer, his warm breath caressing her lips.

"You are so beautiful, Stella." His gaze moved from her mouth, which he'd been staring at while he talked, to the top of her head. His sky blue eyes held hers for a heartbeat then slowly moved down her cheek to rest again on her lips. His mouth hovered over hers, his mustache tickling. She held still, her lungs screaming for air, and waited. She blinked, and he moaned, his lips crushing hers.

Her heart raced as emotion and need took over. She reached up and slid his hat off, letting it drop to the floor. She ran her fingers through his dark brown hair, the strands as soft and thick as she'd imagined. Heat pooled deep inside her. This time it was her groan that slipped through her lips as his hands ran down her arms, lightly touching the outsides of her breasts, and coming to a rest around her waist. His fingers dug into the tender skin as his kiss deepened.

Stella's heart soared while her husband's kisses and gentle caresses healed the ache that had filled her body only minutes before. She lay in bed every night, thinking of the first kiss they'd shared, knowing it might be her first and last. Her body hummed, and she prayed he would someday love her like she loved him. She never wanted this feeling to stop.

A throat cleared behind them, and Travis dropped his hands and stepped away, bending to scoop his hat off the floor and settling it back on his head. She kept her back toward whoever it was, not wanting anyone to see how mortified she was by Travis's reaction—as if he couldn't get away from her fast enough.

"Sorry to interrupt, Mr. Stone, but the missus and I just wanted to thank you for having such a nice hotel. Food's real good too, Mrs. Stone. We're leaving on the early train in the mornin', and wanted to let you know we'll spread the word about this place." There was a moment of awkward silence, and she heard a woman's soft whisper. "Well, that was all I wanted to say. Good night to both of you."

"Same to you, Mr..."

"Allen," Stella whispered.

"Mr. Allen," Travis finished. After the couple left, he gave her a quizzical look. "How'd you know who it was without seeing him?"

"He never addresses his wife by her name, only missus. I don't know that I ever heard what her name was. She's always hiding behind him like she's scared of everything, but he seems nice. Polite." She wiped her sweaty palms on her apron. Untying it, she hung it over the hook and walked away from him. Stepping into the hall, she let her hand rest on the doorframe a moment, her head turned slightly. "I made chicken and dumplings with carrots, if you're hungry."

Travis stared after Stella and rubbed his aching chest. Her tears had broken something inside of him, a barrier he'd erected around his heart during his miserable childhood so long ago. She reminded him of everything he'd lost—everything he had to lose now.

He slowly walked into the dining room, filled his bowl,

and sat down. He ate without really tasting it, although he knew it was probably delicious. Everything Stella made was delicious. A few of her dishes even rivaled Mabel's over at O'Darbys. He watched her from across the room as she smiled at whatever Levi had said. The kid's answering grin made his own mouth turn up. She was amazing with Levi, too. He'd meant what he told her in the kitchen. He was very thankful for what she'd done for the kid—more thankful than she'd ever know.

Growing up, he'd kept everyone at arm's length, never letting people get too close for fear of being hurt again. It was a vow he thought he'd never break. Until now. He understood more than anyone how Levi felt—the loneliness he carried within himself, knowing there was no one out there who loved him. No one to wipe away his tears or take care of him when he was sick. Those were things Travis had always wished for, things his mother had never done for him.

He watched his wife's movements, slow and precise as she slid the side of her fork into her chocolate cake, peeling away one bite at a time. But watching her mouth as each bite disappeared, her lips sliding over the tines of the fork, her tongue licking away the tiny bit of frosting on the side of her mouth…that drove him crazy. By the time she'd finished eating, he was hard and aching, wishing for something he had no right to wish for. He wanted her—more than he'd ever wanted anyone or anything before. She turned, her green gaze piercing his.

He was so focused on his wife, he didn't hear anyone else come into the room until Tom and Ben slid their chairs out and set their own bowls on the table.

"When I heard what Stella was makin' for supper, I couldn't get it out of my head," Ben chuckled. "I think my stomach growled all day."

Tom nodded. "Mine too. That chocolate cake looks mighty fine, too."

Levi hopped up and cut three large slices, setting the cake-filled plates in front of each man. "Miss Stella let me help her—showed me how to put on the frosting."

Tom nodded, made quick work of the main dish, and wiped his mouth. Pushing his empty bowl away, he reached for the plate and turned it around as if studying it. "Yep, shows real mastery. You've got the touch, young man. Not too many can frost their first cake and have it look as nice as this one."

Levi's face shone with pride, and he puffed out his chest. "Go on, take a bite. You gotta try it!"

All three of them raised their forks at the same time. Travis didn't know about his own face, but he knew that Ben and Tom's looks of contentment as they chewed were equal to the sensation filling him. Levi was right: the cake was the best he'd ever had. Once finished, they all sat back with groans, their hands resting on their full stomachs.

"No one better tell my wife about this. I told her I'd eat when I got home later. She's not going to be very happy with me. Maybe I'll just tell her I'm coming down with a stomach ailment. She always leaves me alone when I tell her that."

Stella laughed as she picked up their plates. "Tom! That's a terrible thing to do. Just tell her you stopped by to make sure nobody had bothered us again, and I insisted you eat something."

Tom frowned thoughtfully. "You know, that just might work." He stood, hat in hand, and leaned in, giving her a quick peck on the cheek. "You're an amazing woman, Stella Stone. An amazing woman." He shoved his hat on his head while Ben did the same, and nodded first at Levi, then Travis. "I'll stop by in the morning—we need to have a little powwow about an acquaintance of yours."

Travis frowned. "Mine? I don't know anyone in town, other than you, Ben, and a few others. Who are you talking about?"

Tom shook his head, sliding his gaze sideways to Stella then back to his before she saw. "It's nothing that can't wait 'til morning." He smiled at Levi. "You did a fantastic job, Levi. Make sure you stay close to Stella and keep helping her like a good boy, you hear?" Levi paused at the sheriff's words, the almost empty pot in his hands. He nodded, and without a word, followed Stella from the room.

Tom glanced at Travis then over at Ben. "I'll be waiting for you outside."

Ben waited until the front door closed. "I'm not going into details right now. Tom can do that tomorrow morning. But you need to keep your eyes and ears open. And you need to tell him everything, Travis. He's already starting to put the puzzle pieces together. I meant what I said earlier; it will go better for everyone if he hears the story from you—and you're running out of time."

"I don't—"

Ben held up his hand. "That's all I'm going to say about it. The sooner the better, you hear?"

Travis nodded, his eyes narrowing thoughtfully as he watched his friend leave. What had happened since he'd left the stable for the two men to get worried so fast? He shrugged to himself, and grabbed the platter with what was left of the cake and carried it to the kitchen, along with the clean plates, bowls, and utensils.

As Stella washed the dishes and Levi dried, the boy chattered away about cooking, riding, and anything else that popped into his head. Stella, with her usual patience and animation, egged him on. When they were finished and the kitchen spotless, Levi's shoulders drooped.

Stella gave him a long hug and kissed the top of his head,

something he'd seen her do more and more. "Go on and get ready for bed. If you like, I'll be up in a minute to tuck you in."

He gave her a tired grin. "I'd like that." Without another word, he ran up the stairs.

"He must be tired if he can't raise his feet up enough to keep from making all that noise," Travis said as he stared into the hall, as if he could actually see Levi.

Stella chuckled. "My brothers made the same noise when they were extra tired. He'll grow out of it, just as they did."

He trailed behind her up the stairs. "How old are your brothers?"

"Riley's twelve and Wyatt is ten. I have an older brother, Alex…well, he's really my uncle, but I've always thought of him as a brother. He's twenty-five."

"You're nineteen—that's quite a spread of years between siblings." He stopped at Levi's door, his hand holding the doorknob.

"My mother, Lucie, was a mail-order bride too, and married my father when I was six years old. My two younger brothers are their sons."

He opened the door but stayed in the hall as she tucked the covers around Levi, who was already asleep, his soft snores loud enough to hear from where he stood. Stella glanced over at him and grinned. His own mouth curled up in response. The kid slept as hard as he worked. At that moment, Travis couldn't have been prouder.

Stella crept from the room, softly turning the knob as she closed the door. "He's such a good boy."

For some reason, Travis didn't want the evening to end. "Would you like a cup of cocoa before bed? I usually drop right off to sleep if I drink a cup before turning in."

Her cheeks turned a pale pink, but she gave him a shy nod. "I would love that. Thank you."

He had her sit on the small sofa in the lobby, which gave them a good view of the street and the hills circling the town, while he made their cocoa. Taking a seat beside her, they sipped their drinks quietly. This was another first for him, but he didn't want to admit how much he enjoyed it. Once he started admitting things like that, it would only be harder when he left.

CHAPTER 12

Travis bit back a smile as Stella covered her mouth with a wide yawn. "Tired?"

She nodded then turned in the seat to look at him. "We've been husband and wife for a while now, but I still don't know very much about you. Tell me something about your childhood."

The peace of the night shriveled up like a raisin. "Not much to tell. My mother hated living in New Mexico, and when my father's farm failed, she left. I was on my own by the time I was Levi's age. New Mexico wasn't easy back then, and I did what I had to in order to survive."

"Hmm, sounds familiar. My real mother didn't stay either. She left when I was really young—maybe four or five. Father doesn't like to talk about it, so the only bits I know were told to me by my grandmother. She ran off with a con-man and died about a year later. I can't begin to tell you how lucky I was when Lucie became my mother. Before her, I was so lost and angry, lashing out at everyone. In time though, I learned I was only fighting myself and my broken heart. I blamed myself for her leaving, and couldn't understand why my mother didn't love me enough to stay."

He rubbed the dull ache in his chest. Her story sounded eerily familiar, even down to blaming herself for something she couldn't have changed no matter what she tried to do. For the first time since Anderson's death, he found himself actually wanting to open up and confess to her about his past and the terrible things he'd done. Maybe Ben was right. Living a lie with his feelings bottled up was no different than if he were sitting in a jail cell. It was still a type of prison.

Sitting side by side on the lobby sofa, Stella's head slowly lowered until it lay against his shoulder. She'd fallen asleep. He groaned. Now what was he supposed to do? He mulled over whether to wake her up or not. Finally, he decided he would try to carry her upstairs without waking her. He eased away, holding her head in his hand as he stood. As gently as he could, he pulled her against his chest and wrapped his arm around her shoulders. It took him a bit longer as he struggled with the material of her skirt, but finally managed to slip his other arm beneath her knees.

He made his way up the stairs, smiling at how light she was. Using the hand supporting her knees, he opened her bedroom door and walked inside. Five minutes later, he was still standing beside the bed with his wife in his arms. She let out a soft sigh and snuggled her face into the curve of his neck and shoulder, and he had to bite back a painful groan at what her body was doing to his. He gently laid her on top of the quilt, but she wrapped her arms around his neck and pulled him down to her. She nuzzled her cheek against his; the whisper of his name so soft, he almost didn't hear it.

Turning his face to hers, her lips claimed his. He pulled his head back, but even with the pale yellow light streaming into room from the hall lamps, he could see her well enough.

He'd never noticed how dark her eyelashes were compared to her blonde tresses, or that she had a light dusting of freckles across the bridge of her nose and cheeks. From the story he'd overheard her telling Levi about how rambunctious she'd been as a child, it was easy to imagine her with cute pigtails, rosy cheeks, a wide smile, and an infectious laugh.

"Kiss me again, Travis. Please?"

This time he did moan as he fulfilled her request, drowning in the chocolaty taste of her mouth. Her arms tightened as she pulled him against her. Lying with a woman wasn't new, but the rioting sensations filling his body were. This beautiful, aggravating woman made him want to hug her and run away from her at the same time. The promise he'd made so long ago to never love a woman was disintegrating, and he couldn't do a damn thing about it. She'd somehow managed to wrap herself around his heart so completely, he didn't know where she ended and he began.

Reluctantly, he let her lips go and raised his head. Her gaze was questioning. "Sweetheart, we shouldn't be doing this."

Her mouth turned downward in an adorable pout. "But I've wanted to do this since our wedding."

He frowned. "Really?"

She nodded, placing her hands on either side of his face, her thumbs caressing his cheeks. "You are a good man with a big heart. I couldn't have asked for a more perfect husband."

Her words were like a splash of cold water. He untangled himself from her and scooted to the edge of the bed, clasping his hands together in his lap. He couldn't look at her, afraid of what he'd see. The last thing he wanted was to see disappointment, or worse, disgust in her beautiful eyes. He cleared his throat, trying to find the words to explain why he couldn't be a real husband to her. If she knew the truth about him...when he told her the truth, the affection he'd seen in her eyes would quickly turn to hate.

"I'm so sorry, Stella, but I can't do this...not tonight...or tomorrow. I don't know how to be a husband to you. Can we please keep things the way they have been for just a while longer?"

She let out a soft sigh and rolled over onto her side, facing him. "I do understand, Travis. But getting to know me is only half of what needs to happen. I need to get to know who you are too. I want you to be my husband and my best friend."

He reached over and squeezed her hand, which was lying on her pillow beside her face. "I would like that very much. For the first time in my life, I have two friends. Thank you, Stella."

She gave him a quizzical glance. "For what?"

"For being you."

IT WAS MID-MORNING, and Stella was happier than she'd ever been. She'd made progress in her relationship with Travis, and she couldn't have been more pleased. He'd practically told her their marriage would eventually progress to something more.

The morning was flying by, and their last guest had checked out already. The train wasn't due for another couple of hours, so she and Levi had a little free time until then. She glanced around the lobby, absently running the dust rag across the desktop, wondering what they could do to fill it.

"Miss Stella, I brought us a snack!" Levi announced as he carried one of her serving trays down the hall.

She smiled, noticing the two glasses of lemonade, one plate of cookies, and a second filled with the last of last night's chocolate cake. "I see you're hungry."

"I'm always hungry for cake and cookies—'specially

yours!" He set the tray down in front of her and grabbed two cookies, shoving one in his mouth.

"Excuse me, little man, but we don't eat the entire cookie in one bite. You'll choke."

He scowled doubtfully. "I've never choked before."

She raised her brows and picked a cookie up herself. "You've been lucky then."

He let out a loud sigh. "Fine. I'll take two bites."

"Three."

His eyes narrowed, but he did what she said, albeit grudgingly.

"So, how did you get to Carlsbad after...well—"

"It's okay, Miss Stella. You can say the words—my parents' deaths. Because it was Apaches, the army came to the farm and checked things out. I wanted to stay, but the major wouldn't let me and brought me to town."

She cut a bite from the cake and chewed slowly, then washed it down with a long gulp of lemonade. "So where did you live when you got here?"

While she waited for his answer, he ate the rest of the cake then finished his drink, wiping his mouth with the back of his hand. "Major dropped me off at the sheriff's office and told me to wait. I didn't want to cause any trouble, so I left."

"So where did you go?"

He shrugged. "I hid in an empty building for a while, then someone caught me so I had to move somewhere else. Several of the saloon owners were nice and gave me leftovers whenever they had any. So did Mabel. Her new son's nice, too. He'd sneak me out chicken and bread when he could. After a while, I got tired of sleeping on the ground, so I'd sneak into the loft at Ben's livery and sleep in the hay. It's warmer in the winter, and a lot softer than the ground."

Stella chuckled while trying not to cry, and kept her eyes

lowered so he wouldn't see. "I can imagine." She blinked until the tears dried up and met Levi's brown gaze. "And Travis? How did you meet him?"

He laid his arms on the desktop and rested his chin on his hands. "I'd seen him around town and in the saloon for several weeks. I'd already crawled into the loft at the livery when he came in with his horse. Don't know where he'd been—out ridin', I guess. Travis wouldn't let Ben take care of his horse though. Said he was his best friend, and best friends take care of each other. I waited until Ben went back into his office, then climbed down the ladder and ran after Travis. He went into a boarding house not far from here, so I waited outside until the next morning, then followed him to the saloon. I did this for a couple of days…memorizing his routine, making myself inde...indesp..."

"Indispensable?"

He nodded. "Yeah, indispensable. I got him his food, helped feed and brush his horse, and ran his errands. I did anything I could think of, and stuck to his side like tar. Now he needs me—and won't let me go back to living on my own."

Stella cupped his cheek with her hand. "*I* won't let you go back to that life. I'm sure Travis feels the same way as I do. Your home is here, with us."

His eyes filled with tears, and he sniffed. Stella walked around the front desk and held out her arms. Levi stepped into her embrace, wrapping his arms around her waist. "Th—thank you, Miss Stella."

She ran her hand over his hair, finger combing the wild strands away from his face with one hand, her other rubbing his thin back. "You're welcome, sweetie. You're safe with us. We'll take care of you from now on, no matter what happens, you hear?"

He nodded, but kept his arms around her waist as if he was afraid to let go, so she just held him longer. A movement from across the street caught her eye. Travis stepped off the sidewalk in front of the laundry and slowly crossed the street, his gait easy and relaxed. Amazed, she noticed he even had a smile on his face, and she couldn't help but smile along with him. In her heart, she knew everything she'd ever dreamed of was finally coming true.

TRAVIS OPENED the door and stepped into the lobby and abruptly stopped when he saw Stella holding Levi against her, her fingers combing through his hair. He frowned. "What's wrong?" His heart stuttered. "Did something else happen while I was gone?"

His wife shook her head. "Levi and I were just sharing a mid-morning snack and talking. I told him he didn't have to worry anymore because he was going to stay here with us. I told him we would take care of him from now on."

A burning sensation prickled in the back of his nose and down his throat. He adored Levi, and to know that Stella felt the same way.... Travis had seen with his own eyes how wonderful she was with him, and knowing she felt the same way filled an empty place in Travis's heart.

He pressed his lips together and nodded, then moved closer to the two of them and stood behind Levi. Stella moved her hand to Levi's shoulder, and Travis reached out his hand to ruffle the kid's hair. "Levi, if living here with us is what you really want...." Travis barely raised his arms in time to catch Levi as the kid spun around and jumped into his arms.

"You don't know how much I want to be here with both of you," Levi whispered against his neck.

After a good long hug, Travis lowered Levi back to the

floor. He reached over the boy's head for a cookie, stuffing the entire thing in his mouth. Levi giggled, holding his hand over his mouth and glancing over at Stella, who had a scowl on her face. Travis stopped chewing and frowned. "What?" he said, trying to keep the cookie in his mouth.

"Travis, really? The entire thing?"

Levi giggled again. "I just got in trouble for stuffing the entire cookie in my mouth, too. Miss Stella said I might choke. You could choke too, you know."

He quickly swallowed the cookie, then picked up an almost full cup of lemonade and drank the entire glass. "Mmm, delicious!"

"Want me to get you some more?" Levi asked, already moving toward the kitchen.

"Wait a minute, Levi." He motioned for the boy to come back and waited until he stood beside Stella. "I've asked Miss Smythe to watch over the hotel for the day so we can do something special. We could go on a picnic—if you'd both like to, that is."

Stella met Levi's gaze. They smiled at the same time. "That's a wonderful idea, Travis!" Stella said. "I would love to see more of Carlsbad than the inside of this hotel. I'll put together our lunch, and you two can gather up a basket and a blanket large enough for the three of us to sit on."

In no time, they met back in the lobby; Stella was holding the basket in the crook of her arm, and Levi was grasping the blanket in his. When Travis made the decision to take them on a picnic earlier, he'd borrowed a small wagon from Ben. It was waiting for them out front, and he could hear Deacon stomping the ground in anticipation. He was also going to tell Stella the truth...about his past. By keeping his past hidden, he'd only been fooling himself and couldn't live with that deception any longer.

"As soon as Dorothea arrives, we can begin our little

adventure," Travis said, surprising himself with how excited he was. He couldn't remember a single time in his twenty-seven years that he'd looked forward to anything, much less something as simple as a picnic.

"I know you're in there, Dixon!" Anderson's voice shouted from across the street, where he stood leaning against a support post between the drug store and the Huang brothers' laundry. The wagon jerked forward a few feet as his horse moved out from the line of fire. Deacon had always had an uncanny sense about him, and seemed to know when a gunfight was about to happen. It had saved Travis's life on many occasions.

Travis closed his eyes a moment and let out his breath through clenched teeth. He slid his gun from the holster, but kept it hidden beside his leg as he watched any hope he had for a possible future disappear. He glanced at Levi, who looked at him with wide eyes. He met Stella's questioning gaze, her grip tightening on the basket she now clutched with white knuckles.

"Who is that man, Travis? He came by the hotel a few days ago asking questions...about you."

Levi snickered. "Well, he tried anyway. He wasn't very nice, and Miss Stella punched him in the nose."

She gave a nonchalant shrug of her shoulders, her hard gaze almost daring Travis to say something. "He insulted me, so I hit him. Don't make a big thing of it. The man deserved it."

"I told him it was an improvement." Travis's grin widened as she fought back her own smile.

"Dixon! I meant what I said—your time's up. I'm gonna make you pay for killin' my pa! You can hide behind your wife's skirts, or you can come out here and face me like a man! You should've died out in the desert like I'd planned!"

"You didn't answer me. Who is that man?" Stella asked.

"Now isn't exactly the best time, Stella. That idiot won't wait. At least now I know who shot me."

Her eyes narrowed. "And just what do you think you're going to do? Walk out there and get yourself shot full of holes? Lot of good you'll do us then. If Dorothea was on her way here like you said, she would have heard what that man yelled and went for the sheriff. Wait just a bit longer…it will give you time to explain how this man knows you, and why he believes your name is Dixon."

Travis growled in frustration, but knew Stella well enough to realize she wasn't going to back down. "Fine. Set the basket down on the front desk, and both of you go sit down on the sofa out of his sight. I wouldn't put it past him to shoot at the two of you to get to me." They did what he asked, and he scrubbed his face in frustration. "He thinks my name is Dixon because that's what I used to go by—"

"Have you told your wife who you really are, Dixon? No self-respectin' woman would have anything to do with you if she knew what you'd done. So I guess that makes her a painted lady now, don't it?"

Stella's face reddened. "Well, I never...he just called me a whore again!" She stood, her hands curled in tight fists by her side. "This time I'm going to do more than just punch him in the nose!"

"Don't listen to him, Stella. He wants to rile us up. My guess, he's not alone out there."

"He's not," the sheriff said as he sidestepped from the hall to behind the far end of the front desk so Anderson wouldn't see him. "Two other men are out there, situated on the roofs across the street with rifles aimed at your window. Thankfully, he's too green to realize you have a back door."

"You brought this on yourself, Dixon!" Anderson continued to scream, his voice rising shrilly as his agitation grew, evidenced by his back-and-forth pacing and the way he kept drawing his gun then holstering it again. "Killin' your own pa was a terrible thing to do, but when I found out you killed mine as well, I vowed I'd get you! My pa took you in, treated you like his son—sometimes better'n me. He taught you everything he knew and kept you alive! Remember what he used to say, Dixon? *'Outlaw Trail's a hard life, and you gotta be tough...merciless. It's an eye for an eye out here and if someone else has to die, so be it.'* Remember those words? Pa lived by 'em. He thought you did too!"

Tom's hard gaze settled on Travis's face. "Now I know where I've seen your face. There's a wanted poster back in my office with the name of Sean Dixon on it, and a grainy photo. You've aged quite a bit since then. What was it, fifteen years ago?"

"Depends on what time you're talking about." He ignored Stella's gasp as he continued to stare at the sheriff. "I didn't do the things they said I did, and I only killed two men. Both deserved it. I'd already planned to tell you everything tomorrow morning..."

The sheriff pushed away from the wall he'd been leaning against, anger mottling his face. "Tell me now, then. Who lives and who dies isn't for you to decide! We have a legal system with trials and jails for a reason—"

"And where was this wonderful system when Jason Anderson was holding up that train and threatening to kill the passengers? Where were you or your judge when he grabbed a woman and shot her in the head then threw her newborn babe out of the train?" Travis took a step closer to the sheriff, not caring if those outside could see him or not. "I still hear that woman sobbing, begging for him to let her baby live!" he said between clenched teeth.

"Travis!" Levi screamed.

Travis turned, and Levi darted in front of him as the large window shattered. He saw Levi's body jerk as an explosion of red covered his shirt. He met the boy's wide, pain-filled eyes. Levi fell forward, and Travis caught him, holding him tight against his chest. He couldn't breathe while his fingers searched the boy's neck for a pulse. Behind him, Stella screamed.

CHAPTER 13

Stella took a step, her arms already extended as she reached for Levi, and the men outside fired. Bullets ricocheted around them as she dropped to the floor, fighting her skirts and petticoat as she slipped and slid across the room, seeking cover behind the front desk like Travis and Tom already had.

She finally managed to jerk the material from between her legs where it had bunched up. Once her limbs were freed, she quickly crawled toward Tom, who yanked her behind him as another heavy barrage of gunfire filled the air. She fought against his firm embrace as he held onto her arms and pinned her against him.

"Let me go! I need to help Levi!" she bit out, struggling against the older man, his strength shocking her.

"Travis is doing all he can, ma'am," Tom said, then jerked her further back and away from the encroaching bullets as they ate into the wooden barrier, the only thing now keeping them alive. "Stella, I can't fight you and those men outside at the same time, so sit here and don't move!"

She bit her tongue as he shoved her back against the wall,

knocking her head and shoulders against the wall hard enough to shove the breath from her lungs. Struggling to breathe, she watched as he grabbed his guns and returned their fire, rising and dropping back down in a weird sort of rhythm. When his attention was focused on the men outside and not getting himself shot, she crawled over to Travis and Levi.

Travis glanced up at her as he finished tying a strip of material he'd torn from Levi's shirt, holding another wadded-up piece just above Levi's heart. He grabbed her hand and pressed it on top of the wound. "Keep your hand there and don't move it until we can get him to the doctor—we have to slow the bleeding."

"What are you—"

He pulled his gun from its holster and she flinched, her gaze moving from the gun back up to his face. From the narrowing of his eyes and the firm line of his mouth, she knew he'd seen her reaction. She couldn't help it though… the outlaw's earlier words echoed in her head. Her husband had killed two men. He's said it himself. She bit back a sob and focused her attention on the little boy lying so still beside her. What kind of man had she married? She'd naïvely thought leaving Chattanooga would help her change and be a better person—a sweeter, more docile woman. Instead, here she was, fighting for her and Levi's lives in the middle of a gunfight, and she was married to a killer!

Levi moaned, pulling her attention back to more important matters. He moaned again, and moved his head from side to side. He fought to wake up, his hand reaching out. She reached across his stomach and linked her fingers through his. Leaning closer, she brushed her lips across his clammy forehead, then laid her cheek over the same spot. "Shh, Levi. I've got you. We're going to get the doctor, and he'll make you right as rain, you hear?" She bit back another sob as her emotions threatened to overwhelm her.

"Travis...." Levi whispered.

"Shhh, sweetie. Travis is fine. You are so brave, Levi. You saved his life. He and the sheriff won't let those men get away with this. Sheriff Higgins will make them stop."

"He needs...us," Levi whispered again. "Needs...you."

She swallowed the huge lump in her throat as a surge of anger roiled through her. She forced herself to breathe in and out through her nose until the fury at their situation eased enough for her to answer. "Right now, I want you to focus on getting better. You hear me, Levi? I need you to get better." His head turned sideways as he slipped back into unconsciousness. Her tears flowed freely as she tightened her grip on his hand and softly prayed. "Please Lord, don't take him. He's so young, with a full life ahead of him."

She scrambled to her knees, her back against the inside of the front desk, uncaring about the events unfolding behind them. As carefully as she could, she pulled Levi into her lap, his head resting against her chest as she continued to press against the bullet wound. She heard Tom holler at the men outside, telling them to surrender, which started up another round of shooting. Travis yelled something, but his words were covered by the deafening noise of gunfire.

"Tom!" Ben shouted from the hall. Stella glanced up, her gaze meeting his. The moment he saw Levi's prone body in her tight grip, anger flooded his face.

"Get Stella and the boy over to my house," Tom shouted to him. "Bernie knows how to tend gunshot wounds. She'll keep 'em safe until we're finished here and can get doc over to him!" He and Travis returned a few shots, then stopped to quickly reload. "Got one on the roof."

"I got the other, and another who was between the buildings," Travis added.

Stella's heart felt like a stone inside her chest. He'd killed more men. She knew those men outside were trying to kill them, but her brain simply refused to acknowledge that difference. She'd agreed with what Tom had said earlier about the legal system, that there were laws for a reason. Not for the first time since arriving in New Mexico, she thought the idea of returning home would be best for her. It would definitely be safer. Society was civilized there. Men didn't drunkenly brawl in the streets, and they definitely didn't shoot up the town.

"Stella, you need to let me carry Levi."

She glanced up into Ben's worried face. She hadn't even realized he'd moved from the hall to her side. Silently, she nodded, and let the gentle man take Levi from her, his own large hand covering the blood-soaked bandage.

"Keep down as low as you can and stay right behind me. We're going to go out through the kitchen door. I've got my wagon parked on the street behind us. Once we're out of the house, run like there's a pack of wolves nipping at your heels, you hear me?" he asked. She nodded again, not trusting her voice, and hoped her shaky legs would be able to run.

Ben rose with a nod toward Tom. The men began firing their weapons as they ran down the hall. Stella hesitated, glancing back at the man she'd thought she knew. As if sensing her appraisal, Travis turned his head, his hard gaze hitting hers.

"Go!" he yelled. "Get out of here!"

Turning on her heels, she took off after Ben, who was almost to his wagon. Hiking her skirts almost up to her knees, she took off, running faster than she ever had. Time slowed, and it seemed like it took her forever to reach the wagon. Finally, she climbed into the front and grabbed the reins, which were loosely tied to the tall lever beside her.

She gave Ben a quick glance. "Ready? I'll need you to tell me where I'm going."

One corner of his mouth rose, and his eyes filled with an intense gleam. "I didn't know a woman could run that fast...and in skirts too! You are one helluva woman, Stella Stone." He nodded for her to go and made a clicking sound with his tongue. "One helluva woman."

In any other circumstance, she would've beamed with pride at his praise. But right now, all she cared about was saving Levi. She drove the wagon, trying to avoid any bumps or rocks that would jolt him. Following Ben's directions, she made the short trip to the sheriff's house and was surprised to find a woman—the sheriff's wife, she assumed—already standing in the doorway as if she expected them.

Once inside the house, they got Levi settled into a bed, and Stella watched the woman remove the makeshift bandage from around his thin chest. When she saw the damage left behind by the bullet, the room swam. She bit the insides of her cheeks and forced her gaze back to what the sheriff's wife was doing.

"I know we haven't been formally introduced, Mrs. Stone, and I wish it were under better circumstances. My name is Bernice Higgins, but you can call me Bernie. Out here, Bernice sounds so stodgy and formal." Bernie lifted her brown gaze to hers. "I could use another set of hands."

Stella pulled in a deep breath and pushed her shaky body away from the wall, forcing her feet to move across the wood-planked floor until she was on the other side of the bed. "What...what do you need me to do? I'm afraid I don't have much skill when it comes to caring for wounds. A stomach sickness or cold, I have no difficulties dealing with at all. But this...." She held out her hands, palms up. She'd never felt so helpless.

"Any minute now, Ben will show up with hot water and

fresh rags. He's had to bring the sheriff home a time or two with a few more holes than this in his body that needed tending. The only thing I'll need your help with is keeping the child as still as possible. I'm going to have to probe the wound and get the bullet out, if possible, then sew him up." Her long fingers brushed back a lock of Levi's hair from his forehead.

The woman was right. Not two seconds after she said it, Ben showed up and set the steaming bowl of water with several clean rags on the nightstand beside the bed. He then left, the front door shutting behind him. Stella watched as the woman lovingly cared for Levi, her movements sure and tender. She had to hold Levi down only a couple of times, but she whispered to him, and he slowly calmed back down. Once the bullet had been removed and the large hole stitched closed, she sat back, finally able to breathe again.

The sheriff's wife looked to be a bit older than her own mother, but she was still a very striking woman. Her beautiful red hair was streaked with gray and pulled up in a fashionable knot on top of her head. Tiny curls ringed her face, giving her a youthful look. Her skin was sun-kissed, and she could see tiny laugh lines at the edges of her eyes and mouth. Stella immediately liked her.

"Thank you for helping Levi."

"Oh, *pshaw*. It's nothing, dear. I've been married to a man who is constantly putting himself in the line of fire, so I've gotten a lot of practice at doctoring—whether I wanted to or not. Fortunately for him, and now this young man, I'm good at it." She rinsed her hands in the water and dried them with a clean towel. "Now, how about you and I drink a nice calming cup of tea and get to know each other a bit better?"

Stella bit her lower lip and looked at Levi, not wanting to leave him.

"Thankfully, he will be sleeping for a while. Besides, we'll be in the next room and can hear him if he stirs. When Tom is able to get the doctor here, the boy will be given something for the pain, which will keep him asleep so his little body can begin healing." She walked to the door and gave Stella another smile. "Now, how about that tea?"

Stella nodded and followed her into the next room. She hadn't noticed any of her surroundings when she'd first arrived, her attention focused only on Levi. She found herself sitting in a cozy parlor with lace valances over the two open windows with a nice breeze moving through the room. The light green sofa where she sat was small, with a pretty cream doily lying across the back. There were two cherry wood tables at each end, and a matching high-backed chair sharing the table at the other end of the room.

Bernie returned and placed a silver tray holding a pretty off-white porcelain tea service on the table in front of them. Sitting beside her, Bernie poured the steaming liquid into each cup. She handed Stella one cup then picked up the other, softly blowing the hot tea before taking a small sip. "Mmm. Nothing better than tea for calming frayed nerves, don't you think?"

Stella smiled. "My grandmother always said the same thing."

"Well, of course she did. Your grandmother sounds like a very smart woman."

Stella's smile widened. "She always said that too…especially after arguing with her husband."

They finished their tea in silence. After returning the cups to the tray, Bernie leaned against the back of the sofa, her body partially facing Stella. In the distance, they could still hear occasional gunshots.

"Now, tell me what all the ruckus in town is about. Tom knew there was going to be trouble, but I was hoping he would be wrong. Never is, of course, but a wife can always hope."

"Everything happened so fast…it's all a bit confusing. One minute, my husband, Levi, and I were leaving for a picnic. The next, Levi was shot when he bravely jumped in front of Travis, and I found out I don't really know my husband at all."

"Travis is your husband?" She frowned. "That wouldn't be Travis Stone, the gambler…would it?"

Stella nodded. "I found out just after I got here that he'd requested a mail-order bride to help run his hotel. If I'd known that, I wouldn't have accepted." She glanced at the open doorway to Levi's room. "I am so very glad I did. To not have known Levi…."

Bernie smiled. "You love him like your own."

Stella nodded. "He's so smart, and he helps me without being asked. More importantly, he has such a large heart just waiting to love and be loved. I can't imagine not having him in my life." Tears filled her eyes and she blinked furiously, willing them away. Falling apart right now wouldn't do her or Levi any good.

"And what about your husband?"

Stella stared at her hands clasped tightly together in her lap. "I don't know—I thought I loved him, too. Before today, anyway. But now…." She sighed. "Maybe it would be better if I returned to my family in Chattanooga."

"What a wonderful place! I have very fond memories of my visit there as a child. I traveled with my mother and father to visit his sister whose husband had gone missing. I'd completely forgotten about that until now."

Stella frowned. "Her husband was missing?" How many women from Chattanooga could there be whose husband disappeared? The pounding in her chest quickened. "What was her name—your father's sister?"

Bernie thought a moment, her elbow propped against her wrist as her finger tapped her chin. "I believe her name was Martha—" Stella covered her mouth with a sob. Bernie frowned, concern filling her eyes. "My dear, whatever is the matter?"

"My grandmother's name was Martha, and her husband left her. We found out years later that he'd been killed in a fight out west."

Bernie's eyes widened. "Your grandmother?" She stood and hurried across the room, pulling a book from a small shelf that was hanging in the corner. Sitting down again, she flipped through the pages until she found what she'd been searching for. "I know this would have been long before you were born, but could this be your grandmother?" She handed Stella the small album.

She stared at the familiar face and smiled. She traced her grandmother's serious expression as tears welled in her eyes again. "She always had a smile on her face, and loved to laugh. I have such wonderful memories of her as I grew up." She sniffed and met Bernie's tear-filled gaze. "I guess that makes us family?"

"Oh, my dear, yes. Yes, it does." Bernie reached across the sofa and pulled Stella into her warm embrace. After a few minutes of happy sobbing, Bernie let her go to dab at her eyes with a handkerchief she pulled from the cuff of her sleeve. She handed Stella another handkerchief stuffed inside her other sleeve.

They continued talking, stopping only long enough to check on Levi, who was still asleep. She told Bernie about her life, her family, and how happy her grandmother was when she remarried. Suddenly, Stella's stomach let out a loud growl. "Oh my. Well, that was rude." She laughed, then noticed the sun was now hanging just above the horizon. "Breakfast was quite a while ago, I'm afraid." She stilled, listening to the silence. "The shooting has stopped."

"The last shot was about an hour ago. I expect the men to return any moment." She rose and hurried into the kitchen, pulling food out of the pie safe. "Wouldn't do to let my husband go to bed hungry after working so hard to save everyone, now would it?"

"May I help?"

"Oh, there's really no—"

"Please, Bernie. I would really like to do something to get my mind off things."

"Well, okay then. You can slice the bread while I cut up a few tomatoes and cheese. Whoever finishes first will get the honors of slicing the meat."

Stella chuckled. "Sounds good."

Bernie handed her a knife and cutting board, then began cutting thin slices of tomato and laying them artfully on a small plate. "While we're doing this, tell me more about your husband. What makes you so sure you don't know him?"

"Well, for starters, he lied. I found out today he has a different name, and used to travel the Outlaw Trail. Whatever that is. And he's killed two men—one of them was his own father!" She forced herself to slow down and pay attention to what she was doing, keeping the knife slow and steady as she sawed through the newly baked loaf of bread.

"Oh dear. Well, that is a dilemma. Did he explain why he did those things?"

Stella frowned, the knife stopping halfway through the next slice as her stomach clenched. "Well, no, but he didn't have a chance because that's when the shooting started." She finished the slice and laid the knife on the cutting board. "But what reason could he have to kill his own father? He did explain why he killed the other man. Evidently, the man was the leader of a group of outlaws, and they were robbing the train Travis was on. Travis tried to stop him from killing a young woman and her baby, but he didn't want to take a chance at hitting them by accident. The man shot the woman and threw her baby from the train, and Travis killed him."

"Your Travis sounds very much like my Tom. He would've done the same thing, sheriff's badge on his chest or not. Remember, child, that there's always two sides to every story—and sometimes even more than that depending on how many people are involved." Bernie pulled a thick chunk of meat from the icebox and began slicing. "Now, tell me how young Levi in there joined your little family. The last I knew, he was hiding out in the livery and eating whatever he could find."

Stella chuckled. "That's exactly what he was doing—until Travis rode into town. Levi told me he overheard Travis talking to Ben at the livery. Levi decided to follow Travis like a shadow after hearing him say his horse was his best friend, and that best friends take care of each other."

"Well, then. You have your answer, Stella."

CHAPTER 14

Stella shook her head, giving her new friend a quizzical frown. "What are you talking about?"

"What kind of man would talk about his horse that way, or take care of an orphan, making sure he had a meal every single day and clothes to wear? What kind of man would stand up to someone like that outlaw as he robbed the train, to defend perfect strangers, putting his own life in danger?"

The front door banged open, startling them. They rushed into the other room, stopping abruptly at the sight in front of them. Tom and Ben stood, hats in hand, covered head-to-toe in what looked like black soot.

"Tom Higgins, whatever in the world happened to you?" Bernie glanced at Ben with a crooked smile. "Hello, Ben."

"Hiya, Bernice. Sorry to barge in like this, but Tom said you wouldn't mind...."

Stella stepped forward, her heart beating a painful rhythm against her ribs. "Where's Travis? Is he all right?"

Tom nodded. "He's fine. He's resting as comfortably as he can in my jail. How is young Levi faring?"

"He'll be good as new in a few days—no need to round up

the doctor either. And Ben, of course I don't mind," Bernie said. "Dear me, but you two are a mess." Giving them a wide berth, she moved around them and opened the door. "Both of you, out on the front porch. Strip down to your long johns, and I'll bring you both a change of clothes."

Ben shook his head and took a step back. "But ma'am—"

"No ma'aming me, Ben Caden. I will not have you nor my husband traipsing through this house like that, dirtying everything up. Now do as I say, or neither one of you will get any supper."

Stella shook her head. Bernie was a force to be reckoned with. Her small grin widened. For the first time since her grandmother's death, she felt like a little piece of her was still alive as she watched Bernie take charge. In less than ten minutes, they were all seated around the table eating sandwiches.

Stella's hunger had disappeared after what Bernie had said about Travis. She picked at the other half of the sandwich on her plate. It bothered her that he wasn't here. It was like something was missing. Could Bernie be right? She'd seen the way Travis's eyes turned guarded at the mention of his family or his past. She knew his mother had left them when he was little, but what else had he left out?

"So are you going to tell us what happened?" Bernie asked.

"We got everybody but Anderson...I'm embarrassed to say this, but he got one over on us. We were holding him off, or so we thought, when he somehow threw burning rags onto the roof and into the upstairs rooms on both ends of the hotel. Didn't take long until the whole place went up in flames." Tom met Stella's horrified gaze. "I'm sorry, Stella, but...."

Ben nodded. "We couldn't get up there fast enough to save any of your belongings. Travis tried...almost killed himself trying to run down the hallway to your room. Floor caved in on him, but luckily the desk in his office broke his fall. Oh, he'll have a few bruises, but he's alive."

"Thank God," Stella whispered.

Tom tilted his head, his steady gaze studying her face. "I figured you'd be halfway back to Chattanooga when you found out what he'd done, and that he'd lied to you."

Stella smiled at Bernie. "If it hadn't been for your wife, I probably would have caught the first train out of town—as soon as Levi was okay to travel, at least."

Bernie set a plate of cookies in the center of the table, then poured everyone coffee. "Tom, you are never going to believe what Stella and I have discovered!"

Tom groaned. "Do I want to know?"

His wife scowled at him and shook her head, but her smile instantly returned when she glanced at Stella, then back at her husband. "Do you remember me telling you about my Aunt Martha? My father's sister?"

He shrugged. "Well, not really."

"Oh, you remember. She was the one whose husband disappeared, and we took a trip to see her. You are never going to believe this, but Stella is Aunt Martha's granddaughter!"

Tom's face went blank as his gaze moved back and forth between the two women. "You know, now that I see you two so close together, there *is* a good resemblance." He stood and moved around the table, pulling Stella into a hug. "Welcome to the family, young lady!" He pulled his wife into the hug, squeezing them both. "What a good ending to a perfectly terrible day."

THE MORNING CAME FASTER than Stella liked. She'd gotten little to no sleep…first with worrying about Levi, then not being able to stop thinking about Travis. She'd tossed and turned, finally giving up as the first rays of pink and orange light appeared in the sky. She dressed and went to Levi's room.

She sat on the side of his bed, watching the steady rise and fall of his chest. Both her head and heart ached as she thought about what she was going to do now. Bernie had said there were two sides to every story. She of all people should know that from many of her past experiences. Exhausted from all the worry and anxiety from the last twenty-four hours, she inched her way onto the mattress and lay beside Levi. She laid her hand over his heart, the strong, steady beat reassuring her more than anything else that he was going to be all right. Her eyes drooped, then finally closed.

The banging of pans woke her with a jerk. She sat up and stretched before touching the back of her hand to Levi's cool face. She kissed him on the forehead, then went in search of Bernie, following the scent of frying bacon to the kitchen. Stella watched her pull long strips of delicious smelling bacon from the pan, transferring them to a nearby plate. Bernie then scooped up spoonfuls of scrambled eggs into a pretty yellow bowl with small orange flowers along the rim, then turned and set the bowl on the table before noticing Stella.

Bernie smiled. "I went to your room to wake you, and much to my surprise, you weren't there. When I saw you asleep beside Levi, I didn't have the heart to disturb you."

Stella sighed. "I'm grateful. I couldn't sleep at all last night, and finally rose at dawn. I only meant to check on him, but fell asleep instead."

"Nothing wrong with that. Your presence probably comforted him as well."

They ate in companionable silence. As they sipped their

coffee, Stella remembered a question she'd meant to ask the day before. With everything that had happened, she'd forgotten.

"Bernie, do you and Tom have children?"

Bernie set her cup on the table. "We had our beautiful daughter for four days. She's buried with my parents in the family cemetery."

"I'm so sorry. I didn't mean to bring up sad memories."

Bernie smiled. "For me, they are beautiful memories. I never got pregnant again, but I don't think Tom minded. He took Lilly's death hard. Now, my dear, tell me what you've decided to do about your young man."

Stella sighed with a half-hearted shrug. "I don't know what to do."

"Well, maybe since he can't go anywhere, you can march down to that jail and start asking him questions."

Stella smiled. "What a wonderful idea!" She jumped up and gave her new cousin a hug. "Bernie, you're brilliant!"

Bernie laughed. "Yes. Sadly, only you and I know that little fact." Bernie shooed her from the kitchen toward the door. "Go. Talk to your husband. Find out his side of the story."

Stella arrived at the jail. She trailed her hand along the orange-tan adobe, the texture slightly rough against her skin. A covered porch with rounded timbers sticking out of the front took up most of the building's facade. She walked inside and found herself in what she assumed was the sheriff's office. There was a small desk, a chair, and a large map on the wall of New Mexico. Otherwise, the room was empty.

She walked over to the map, wondering where the sheriff was, when she heard the low murmur of voices. Turning around, she noticed the partially opened door behind her. Her steps slowed as she drew closer. She recognized Travis's voice. In spite of everything, the sound washed over her and calmed her jumbled nerves. She stood beside the door and listened.

"We have a few things to settle, young man. First, what's your real name? Is it Sean Dixon or Travis Stone?"

Stella held her breath, waiting for his answer.

"Both are, sort of."

"Explain."

"Jason Anderson found me when I was thirteen...starving, with no home or family. He took me in and treated me like his son. From the beginning, though, there was something off about the man, and I never really trusted him. When he first asked me my name, I gave him my middle name, Sean, and my mother's maiden name, Dixon. My real name is Travis Sean Stone."

"See? Now that wasn't so hard, was it?"

She smiled when she heard Travis growl in frustration. Surprisingly, she was happy. He'd given his real name when they'd married.

"You told me about killing Jason, which I've ruled as a justified killing, especially since he was the leader of one of the most notorious and dangerous outlaw bands running this area. However, I still need to hear about your father."

The silence in the small building grew until it began to close in around her. She chewed on her lower lip, willing Travis to explain so she could begin trusting him—and her own heart—again.

"Fine, be stubborn. It's not going to do you any good. I'll just keep asking until you tell me. Explain why your name is on a wanted poster for several robberies."

"I told you before, I was only the lookout. If I saw someone even resembling a lawman, I was supposed to warn the men. That's all I ever did. For all I know, someone saw me and assumed I was robbing the bank too. Listen, I knew what they were doing was wrong, but I also owed them for saving my life. Hell, I was only a kid!"

"Alright. Now, let's go back to your parents. What happened to your mother?"

"She left pa and me when I was ten. My father was better at drinking than farming. He lost the farm, and my mother left. Haven't heard from her or seen her since, and don't really care to. A man from the bank came out and felt sorry for me when he saw...when he saw how we were living. He even gave me some coin to buy food. He knew my father would only spend it on alcohol. The beatings began when I turned eleven. I learned to stay away from him on his worst days.

"I guess I got a bit complacent and wasn't paying attention one day. I'd just turned thirteen. I celebrated by catching a rabbit—the first food I'd eaten in about a week, other than a few pods of fruit that had fallen from a cactus the day before. I was outside skinning the rabbit when the first blow came. He kicked me across the yard, slamming me into a large cholla. Hurt like a son of a bitch, but thankfully, the spines were short. After another hour of being hit, my broken nose was so swollen I could only breathe through my mouth, and my left eye wouldn't open. I could only see enough with my right eye to detect his shadow as he came for me again. By that time, I was lying halfway through the door of the hovel we lived in. I reached inside, trying to find something to defend myself with. My hand wrapped around the grip of his pistol, which was usually hanging on a peg by the door. I did the only thing I could think of to save my own skin, Tom. I shot him. Shooting was the one thing my father did well. Better than that, even. His shots were accurate and deadly. And he taught me."

Mesmerized by his story, horror and revulsion filled her, along with a feeling so familiar and necessary to her very being. With everything she was, she loved him. Before she realized what she was doing, she found herself standing in the narrow doorway, tears streaming down her face. "Travis," she whispered in a broken sob.

Travis jumped up, his face a mixture of anger and shame. "Stella—what are you doing here?"

She glanced at Tom, who stood from the wooden chair he'd been straddling. He pulled the key from a hook behind him and unlocked the cell door, pushing it slightly open. He rehung the key and turned, laying a heavy hand on her shoulder for a moment, then left the room. She heard the front door close softly behind him.

She took a shaky breath and walked toward the iron door. She opened it as far as it would go and stepped inside. She faced her husband. Eyes closed, he stood stiffly with his forehead pressed against the bars, his tanned skin flushed. "Travis."

He shook his head and wrapped his hand around one of the bars, but never looked at her. "You weren't supposed to hear that."

"Why? Did you think I'd turn my back on you because your father beat you? Because your mother left you when you were young? My mother left me too, at a much younger age." She took a step closer, willing him to look at her, but he didn't. "I thought you'd like to know that Levi will be okay. Bernie, the sheriff's wife, got the bullet out and sewed him up."

"Tom told me when he got here this morning."

She took another step toward him. "What about us, Travis? You, me, and Levi? I thought we were becoming a family. Are you ready to just throw that away because you're ashamed of your past?" She chuckled. "I've only told you and Levi a few things about mine, but believe me, I was a heathen child. That was actually my nickname. I ran people's livestock off their property, I tortured my classmates—especially if they were boys—and I even shot a neighbor's dog."

Finally, he lifted his head, a shocked expression on his face. "You shot a dog? How old were you?"

She stared back, wanting to laugh, but keeping any emotion from showing. "Six."

His lips quivered, his nose flaring as he tried not to laugh. She smiled, a chuckle beginning low in her throat. He laughed, loud and hard, until he couldn't stand straight anymore, his arms clutching his stomach. Finally, their laughter died away. Pulling in a deep breath, he leaned his head back against the bars, sadness in his eyes. "I should have never brought you into all of this, Stella. For that, I am so very sorry. When Levi came up with the mail-order bride plan, I thought it would be simple: bring in a woman, and have her run the hotel." He held her gaze. "I never planned on falling in love with her, though."

She gasped and covered her mouth with her hand. A feeling like nothing she'd ever felt before poured through her like a raging river. All the stress and worry was washed away, and what remained was a love so pure and powerful it took away her breath and filled her heart so full she ached from it.

"The hotel's gone. We lost everything."

She reached across the small space separating them, and brushed what looked like a smudge of soot from his cheek with the pad of her thumb. He smelled like smoke and man. He smelled like home. "So we start over—together."

Before he could stop her, she flew into his strong arms. They wrapped around her, holding her tight against him. "Do you know when I fell in love with you?" she whispered, nuzzling his neck and loving the feel of his whiskers as they rubbed against her skin.

She heard his sharp inhale, then his breath rushed out in a *whoosh.* The next thing she knew, he was twirling her around in the small cell. Finally, he slowed to a stop, sliding her body down his until she felt the floor touch the tip of her toes. Holding her face in his hands, he smiled and lowered his lips to hers in a soft kiss. Pulling away, he reached into his pocket and pulled out a necklace, holding it in front of her face.

She gasped, reaching for it. "How? I thought I'd never see this again."

He helped fasten the gold chain around her neck. Her finger caressed the diamond now resting on her collarbone. He gave her another quick kiss. "When?"

She frowned. "Huh?"

His smile widened. "When did you fall in love with me?" He wiped the remaining wetness from her cheeks.

She rested her cheek against his heart, listening to the heavy *thud, thud, thud,* and said a quick prayer of thanks for giving her back her husband. "The night you and Levi cooked. You were so kind and patient, no matter what he did. You encouraged him to be a child again." She raised her face to his. "Our child. Do you know what you and Levi have taught me, Travis? I've learned that our past shapes us, but it doesn't define who we are…with a little bit of love, we become who we're meant to be."

He nodded. "I'm so sorry—"

She put her finger over his lips and smiled. "No more talking, Mr. Stone. More kissing." She rose to her tiptoes and pressed her lips to his. "Definitely much more kissing."

~

I hope you enjoyed *The Gambler's Mail-Order Bride.* Turn the page to read the excerpt from the next book in the series, *The Bookseller's Mail-Order Bride,* or use the link to buy it. http://tiny.cc/mobsw-bookseller

I need your help.
Reviews help readers find books, so please click the link to leave a review on Amazon.
BookBub and GoodReads are also great options.
http://www.amazon.com/review/create-review?&asin=B01MS07H4Q

THE BOOKSELLER'S MAIL-ORDER BRIDE

CHAPTER 1

Woodward, Oklahoma Territory, 1907

"Take your grubby hands off me, Clayton Jackson!" Hailey Jefferson yelled, swallowing the panic rising up her throat. The man in question only laughed and pressed her back against the brick wall of the hotel where she'd grown up. She was trapped.

He groped her breast with one hand and leaned forward, slobbering wet kisses along her neck. His whiskey-laden breath burned her nostrils. Her last meal threatened to make an appearance as fear and desperation gripped their icy fingers around her heart.

"Yer not git'n away from me this time. I'm tired of chasin' you. I'm gonna show you just how much of a man I am."

She tried to turn her head away from the stench of his rancid breath as it poured across her face. She opened her mouth to scream again when he let out a loud grunt, slowly sliding to the ground at her feet. She stood with her eyes closed and her body shaking, afraid if she looked, she'd find herself in an even worse predicament.

"Oh laws, Hailey, that was a close one!"

Hailey's eyes flew open and she jerked her head up. Her best friend, Jocelyn Duncan, stood in front of her with a wide-eyed expression, her hand still gripping the neck of a broken bottle. Hailey glanced at the man lying at her feet, a trickle of blood oozing from a gash on the side of his head. "Joss? Thank the good Lord you showed up."

Jocelyn tossed the bottle to the ground and wrapped her hand around Hailey's arm, pulling her down the alley toward the sliver of yellow light spilling over the rocky dirt from the open door of the hotel's back entrance. "Come on! Before someone comes looking for him."

They raced up the back stairwell to the third floor where their rooms were. Hailey pulled out the skeleton key the owner had given her years before and unlocked her door. With a quick glance down one end of the hallway to the other, she shoved Jocelyn inside and locked it behind her.

Jocelyn let out a puff of air and leaned against the door. "Hailey, honey, that was too close a call. I only came downstairs to ask if you were going to stop cooking early like we planned. What if—"

"Don't go there, Joss." Hailey sat down on the edge of her bed, staring at the threadbare rug on the floor beneath her feet. "If you say it..." She bit back a sob, her eyes filling with tears. Tears she refused to shed. Furious, she blinked several times, forcing her eyes to dry up. She threw back her shoulders and lifted her chin. "I'm not staying here any longer." She met Jocelyn's watery green gaze, her best friend's eyes so similar to her own. "And neither are you or Toby."

She stood and pulled the old carpetbag from underneath the bed and shoved her few belongings inside: a tarnished silver brush and the matching mirror, which had a crack down the middle, her only nightgown, and her second gray dress. She fastened the closure and moved in front of Jocelyn, holding the bag's handle with both hands. "Snap out of it, Joss. We need to pack your and Toby's things."

Unmoving, Jocelyn stared at her. "And just *where* do you think we are going to go? This hotel has been your home for most of your life, and now ours. We don't have anywhere else to go and you know it."

Hailey twisted the doorknob and jerked the door open. Grabbing her best friend's arm, she pulled her to the closed door of the room next to hers. Without knocking, she opened it and shoved Joss inside. Toby glanced up from his book, his brows rising as they stumbled into the room.

"Pack your bags. Both of you. We're going to Dollie's ranch."

"It's about time." Toby let out a loud *yahoo* and reached under the bed for their bags. As quickly as Hailey had, he packed their meager belongings. He stopped and turned to face Hailey with a frown, crossing his thick arms over his broad chest. "But why are we suddenly leaving now...in the middle of the night?"

His wife rubbed her hands up and down her thin arms. "Nine o'clock is not the middle of the night. Clayton Jackson tried to accost Hailey again. If I hadn't gone downstairs—"

"And hit him over the head with a bottle of whiskey." Hailey smiled.

"And hit him with a bottle. Well, I don't even want to think about what might have happened," Jocelyn finished, her voice barely more than a whisper.

Toby's lips twitched as he stared down at his wife. "You actually hit him?"

She threw her arms up in the air. "I *had* to! He had Hailey pinned against the wall down in the alley. I grabbed the first thing I saw. Thankfully, Clayton took his bottle with him when he left the saloon; otherwise, I would have had to jump on his back and start whaling on him."

Toby let out a bark of laughter and slapped his knee. "Always knew your pretty red hair would come in handy."

Jocelyn hit him in the shoulder and rolled her eyes. "Oh, please...." She grabbed her bag from the bed and marched over to stand beside Hailey, who loved watching her two best friends battle it out.

They hadn't changed in that respect since they were ten years old. She adored them for it. They were the closest thing to family she had left. Why, Joss was more of a sister than anything else. They even looked alike, with similar features and bright green eyes. Their hair was the only thing about them that was different, with Hailey's being a dark, rich brown to contrast Jocelyn's vibrant auburn.

They quietly made their way through town and headed south toward Dollie Kezer's ranch. They walked the four miles in about an hour, but when they arrived, the house sat in total darkness, the green-painted front door only a dark shadow sitting in the middle of the long covered porch.

Hailey sat on the wooden planks of the porch, her bag in her lap, and leaned on it with her elbows, resting her chin in her hands. "Now what? She's evidently in bed."

Jocelyn sat beside her. "Or away. Didn't she say she was leaving on a trip sometime this month?"

Hailey shrugged, her gaze on the darkness surrounding them.

"One of us could knock, you know," Toby pointed out.

"What if she's asleep? That would be rude," Jocelyn snapped.

"Well, it's better than sleeping on her front porch."

Hailey sighed. "Stop bickering. I'm sure Dollie wouldn't mind if we slept in the barn. We used to do it all the time when we were little. I'm sure it's not that bad now that we're grown."

"How about sleeping in real beds instead?" a soft voice said behind them.

The girls jumped to their feet and spun around. Standing in the open doorway, Dollie's silhouette against the room's dark interior was a stark contrast as she faced them in her white robe, her long brown braid draped over her shoulder.

"What are you three doing here so late?" Her gaze lowered to the bags still clutched in their hands, then rose to meet Hailey's, one sculpted brow rising.

"I'm sorry, Dollie, but we had nowhere else to go. The hotel isn't safe anymore—"

~

Can Alex convince Hailey to continue their marriage by Christmas Eve? To find out, click or go to the link below.

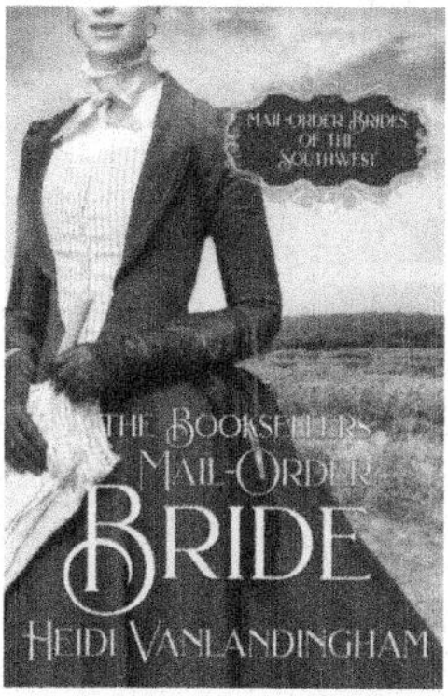

http://tiny.cc/mobsw-bookseller

TRAIL OF INJUSTICE

BOOK 1, WESTERN TRAILS

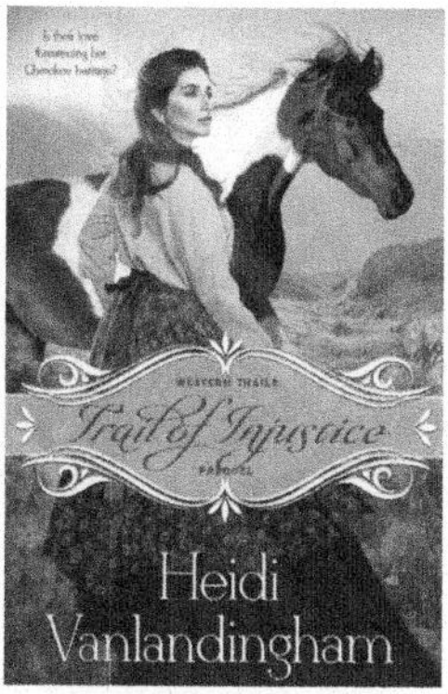

http://tiny.cc/wt-injustice

Water Lily loves working her parent's farm, but she is troubled by the incoming settlers as they move west, stealing what has been under the Cherokee's care for centuries.

Anxious for land and family, Jerrod Santini stumbles into the middle of a plot by local white settlers to steal the Cherokee's silver and gems.

United in their quest to stop them, Jerrod and Water Lily fall in love, a joining that could bring the two opposing sides together or the catalyst that starts a war.

MUSIC AND MOONLIGHT

BOOK 1, MISTLETOE KISSES

http://tiny.cc/mk-mm

Jillian Simpson loves Christmas, but she loves Graham Rogers more and prays one day he will see her for the woman she is and not the orphan girl he left behind.

Graham Rogers once believed Christmas was magical, but life changed him. He returns home to woo Jillian, but his plans are ruined when a woman arrives claiming to be his fiancée and his promised job falls through.

Will the magic of Christmas be strong enough to bring Jillian and Graham together again?

If you love historical romances, sign up for my reader list, and as a thank you, I'll send you the first book, a novella, in my Western Trails series.

To download, go to http://tiny.cc/nl-histwest

ALSO BY HEIDI VANLANDINGHAM

For all Buy Links: www.heidivanlandingham.com

Western Trails series

Trail of Injustice (1)

Trail of Hope (2)

Trail of Courage (3)

Trail of Secrets (4)

Mia's Misfits (5)

Mia's Misfits is also in ABC Mail-Order Bride series

Trail of Redemption (6)

American Mail-Order Bride series &

Prequel to Mail-Order Brides of the Southwest

Lucie: Bride of Tennessee

Mail-Order Brides of the Southwest series

The Gambler's Mail-Order Bride

The Bookseller's Mail-Order Bride

The Marshal's Mail-Order Bride

The Woodworker's Mail-Order Bride

The Gunslinger's Mail-Order Bride

The Agent's Mail-Order Bride

WWII

Heart of the Soldier

Flight of the Night Witches

Natalya

Aleksandra

Of Mystics and Mayhem series

In Mage We Trust

Saved By the Spell

The Curse That Binds

Mistletoe Kisses

Music and Moonlight

Sleighbells and Snowflakes

Angels and Ivy

Nutcrackers and Sugarplums

Box Sets Available

Mail-Order Brides of the Southwest: 3-Book collection

Mistletoe Kisses: 4-book collection

Western Trails: 2-book collection

ABOUT THE AUTHOR

Author Heidi Vanlandingham writes sweet, action-packed stories that take place in the Wild West, war-torn Europe, and otherworldly magical realms. Her love of history finds its way into each book, and her characters are lovable, strong, and diverse.

Growing up in Oklahoma and living one year in Belgium gave Heidi a unique perspective regarding different cultures. She still lives in Oklahoma with her husband and youngest son. Her favorite things in life are laughter, paranormal romance books, music, and long road trips.

She currently writes multiple genres but fixates mostly on paranormal and historical romance.

For more about Heidi: www.heidivanlandingham.com

facebook.com/heidi.vanlandingham.author
bookbub.com/authors/heidi-vanlandingham
goodreads.com/heidivanlandingham
pinterest.com/Hvanlandingham
instagram.com/heidivanlandingham_author

Made in the USA
Monee, IL
30 June 2020

35226229R00111